RABINDRANATH TAGORE

FAREWELL MY FRIEND

RABINDRANATH TAGORE

FAREWELL MY FRIEND

JAICO PUBLISHING HOUSE
Ahmedabad Bangalore Bhopal Bhubaneswar Chennai
Delhi Hyderabad Kolkata Lucknow Mumbai

Published by Jaico Publishing House
A-2 Jash Chambers, 7-A Sir Phirozshah Mehta Road
Fort, Mumbai - 400 001
jaicopub@jaicobooks.com
www.jaicobooks.com

© Jaico Publishing House

FAREWELL MY FRIEND
ISBN 978-81-8495-164-6

First Jaico Impression: 2010
Second Jaico Impression: 2011

No part of this book may be reproduced or utilized in
any form or by any means, electronic or
mechanical including photocopying, recording or by any
information storage and retrieval system,
without permission in writing from the publishers.

Printed by
Repro India Limited
Plot No. 50/2, T.T.C. MIDC Industrial Area
Mahape, Navi Mumbai - 400 710.

Contents

Translator's Note	1
Concerning Amit	4
Collision	21
Retrospect	29
Labanya's Past	34
Aquaintance	43
Intimacy	49
Matchmaking	63

Contents

Labanya Argues	82
Change of Abode	89
Second Sadhana	97
Love's Philosophy	105
The Last Evening	115
Misgiving	128
The Comet	140
Impediment	150
Liberation	165
The End	169
The Last Poem	171

Translator's Note

The original Bengali novel *Shesher Kavita* (lit. Last Poem) was published in 1929. Its modern setting, its playful mocking tone, its challenging style, the author's trick of introducing himself as the butt of the hero's merciless criticism, the brilliant sparkling wit of the dialogue and the final tragic note voiced in the beautiful poem which gives the book its title—all these won for the novel an immediate popularity with the young readers. Some admirers even acclaimed it as the author's best novel; but the enthusiasm of the young, and specially the modern young, must be accepted with considerable caution. The novel is undoubtedly brilliant and entertaining, but to regard it as better than *Gora or The*

Home and the World is to prefer cleverness to genius. However, literary values can never be absolute. To each the pleasure of his choice.

The author draws an amusing picture of an ultra-modern Bengali intellectual whose Oxford education, while giving him a superiority complex, has induced in him a craze for conscious originality which results in a deliberate and frivolous contrariness to all accepted opinion and convention. His aggressive self-complacence, however, receives a shock when as the result of an accidental meeting he falls in love with, and wins in return the heart of a quite different product of modern culture—a highly educated girl of fine sensibility and deep feelings. This love being more or less genuine and different from his previous experience of coquetry, releases his own submerged depth of sincerity, which he finds hard to adjust to the habits of sophistry and pose, practised so long. In the process he manages to strike a new romantic attitude. The struggle makes of him a curiously pathetic figure—one who is being worked against his grain. The tragedy is understood by the girl, who releases him from his troth and disappears from his life. The last poem which she addresses to her lover gives evidence of the depth of feeling of which she was capable.

Much more than the development of the plot of the novel, it is the form of its presentation, the artistry of the author's style, the exquisite poetry interwoven with scintillating, sophisticated prose, the half-lyrical, half-mocking tone of the narrative, which startle the reader and give the novel its distinction. Unfortunately, it is precisely these virtues which, as it were, evaporate in the process of being rendered in an alien medium like English, whose spirit and idiom are so entirely different from those of the original. However, what has been found possible to retain is here presented, with the hope that the reader will not judge the novel without having read the original Bengali version.

Krishna Kripalani

Concerning Amit

Amit Rai is a barrister. When, under the stress of the English accent, this Bengali surname was transformed into Roy and Ray, its beauty no doubt was marred, but its patrons increased. Aiming at a more original name, Amit saw to it that his English friends of both sexes pronounced it as Amit Rayé.

Amit's father had been a formidable barrister. He left enough patrimony to ensure the moral ruin of three successive generations; but somehow Amit managed to withstand the terrific impact of this rich legacy. Without waiting to graduate in the University of Calcutta, he went to Oxford, where he flirted with examinations for seven years. He was too intelligent to be studious. His native wit concealed the gaps in his learning. However, his father had expected nothing extraordinary from him beyond the assurance that the Oxford dye of his only son should be able to stand the native wash.

I like Amit. A fine fellow. I am a new writer with a very limited number of readers, foremost among whom is Amit. He is carried away by the glamour of my style and is convinced that those whose names count in our literary market have no style worth the name. Their literary creations are like the camel in the animal world—neck and shoulders, belly and back, front and behind, uncouth and clumsy; and like the camel they shamble across the bleak desert of Bengali literature with their loose, disjointed gait. This opinion, let me hasten to assure the critics, is not mine.

Amit likens fashion to a mask, and style to the charm of the face. Style, according to him, is for the literary aristocrats, whose ways wait on no will save their own, while fashion is for the underlings who cater to others' taste. For Bankimian style read Bankim's novel *Visha Vriksha* where Bankim is just himself; but for Bankimian fashion read Nasiram's *Manomohaner Mohan Bagan* where the real Bankim has been mutilated. A professional dancing girl exhibits herself under the canvas shade of a public pavilion, but a bride's face must have a veil of Banarasi silk, raised only for the first auspicious glimpse on the wedding eve. Fashion has its canvas and style its Banarasi silk, each special face its shade to match. Style, says Amit, suffers so much neglect in our land simply because our feet dare not stray from the beaten track. A legendary illustration of this truth is the story of *Daksha-Yajna*. Invitations to the sacrificial ceremony were duly sent to Indra, Chandra and Varuna who were the most fashionable gods in heaven. But Siva had a style of his own. So original was he that the spell-mongering priests thought it improper to welcome him. I enjoy hearing such talk from an Oxonian for I believe that my writings are distinguished by style—which is why all my books have attained nirvana, their liberation from rebirth, in the very first edition.

My wife's brother Nabakrishna could not stand these *obiter dicta* of Amit's and would burst out, "To hell with these Oxonians of yours!" He himself was a prodigious M.A. in English literature, of stupendous learning but small understanding. The other day he opined to me, "Amit magnifies the mediocre only to belittle the masters. He loves to beat his drum of insolence and you are his drumstick." Unfortunately this was uttered in the presence of my wife. But it is gratifying to record that even she, his own sister, was not impressed by this indictment. I could see that she endorsed Amit's tastes, though her education had been negligible. The native intelligence of women is amazing.

At times even I am taken aback by the cavalier ease with which Amit runs down well-known English authors. Such authors are what may be called the hall-marked ware freely accepted in the market. It is not necessary to read them to admire them. One has only to praise them to secure the necessary pass marks. Hence Amit too finds it unnecessary to read them since he can with impunity revile them. The fact is that the famous authors seem to him too official and public, like the waiting room at Burdwan station, while the authors discovered by him are his own special reserve, like the saloon in a special train.

Amit is obsessed with style—not only in his literary preferences, but in his dress, outfit and manners as well. His appearance has a distinction which singles him out in any company, not as one of the five but as the absolute fifth which extinguishes the rest. His full, clean-shaven face is dark, smooth and glowing, his manner vivacious, his eyes lively, his smile playful and his movements restless. His retorts flash swift as sparks from flint. He generally wears Bengali dress, for the simple reason that it is not in vogue in his set. His carefully crinkled dhoti is plain and borderless, for that too is "not done" at his age. His tunic is buttoned from left shoulder to right waist and his sleeve-seams are open from cuff to elbow. Girdled round his waist over the dhoti is a broad, maroon-coloured, gold-embroidered band, to the left of which hangs a small bag of Brindaban chintz, carrying his pocket-watch. On his feet is a pair of red-and-white slippers of Cuttack workmanship. When he goes out, a Madrasi border chaddar hangs in neat folds from his left shoulder to his knee; and when he is invited to dinner at a friend's he flaunts on his head the white embroidered cap worn by Muslims of Lucknow. The whole thing is not so much a costume as an uproarious joke. The principle of his English attire is not quite comprehensible, but those who know best affirm that though somewhat loose and baggy it is what is called in England "distinguished". It is not that he affects the odd so much as that he is possessed by a zeal to hold up fashion to ridicule. There are too many young men who have to prove their youth by their birth certificates. Amit's youth is of that rare kind which needs no proof save its sheer, unashamed youthfulness, at once extravagant and irresponsible, like a flood that overflows, letting nothing accumulate, sweeping everything along.

Amit has two sisters whose pet-names are Cissie and Lissie. From head to heel they are absolutely the latest brand—smartly wrapped ware in the showcase of fashion. They fancy high heels and dangle over their lace-trimmed, low-cut blouses beads of amber and coral, while their saris cling and slant serpentwise across their limbs. They trip when they walk, and squeak when they talk; their laughter is measured in a crescendo of squeals; they tilt their heads, smiling winsomely, darting quick sidelong glances; they can look soulful too. Their rosy silken fans constantly flutter about their cheeks, and perching on the arms of their admirers' chairs they tap them with their fans by way of mock protest at their mock impertinences.

Amit's familiarity with the girls of his set is such as to excite the envy of his male acquaintances. He is not insensible to the charms of the fair sex, nor yet apparently responsive to those of any one in particular; the gallantry of his attentions extends to all of them alike. In a word, it might be said of him that he is not affected by women, though he is enthusiastic about them. Amit attends parties, plays cards, loses stakes when he so chooses, and has a way of importuning a bad singer to repeat her performance; and if he sees a girl in an odious-coloured sari he asks for the address of the dealer. He starts a *tete-a-tete* with any casual acquaintance and imports into it a note of intimacy, though everyone knows that this intimacy hides total indifference. The gods are never deceived by a votary who worships many gods and exalts each in turn as the most high, and yet they are pleased. And so the daughters, though their mothers may desperately cling to hopes, have long since discovered that Amit is like the golden hue on the horizon, seemingly at hand but never actually so. His mind hovers over girls without alighting on any one. He ventures so daringly because his intimacies are aimless, and fears no proximities because even if explosives are near he is determined to yield no spark.

The other day at a picnic Amit was sitting beside Lily

Ganguly on the bank of the Ganges. The moon rose above the dark deep stillness of the farther shore. Amit whispered, "Lily, the rising moon on that side of the Ganges and you and I on this side—such a moment will never happen again."

At first Lily's heart gave a momentary leap, but she knew well that the words were true only in the sense that they were true to form—no more to be relied upon than the iridescent colour on a bubble. Shaking herself free from that passing enchantment, Lily laughed and replied, "Amit, what you said is so true that you needn't have said it at all. A frog plopped into the water a moment ago, that moment too will never happen again."

Amit laughed. "There's a difference, Lily, a complete and absolute difference. In this evening hour the jumping frog is an irrelevant, discordant thing. But you and I and the moon, the flow of the Ganges and the stars in heaven, are a perfect and harmonious creation, like Beethoven's Moonlight Sonata. It is as though there were some mad celestial jeweller in the Creator's workshop who makes a lovely, flawless golden ring enwrought with diamond, emerald and sapphire—and no sooner completes it than he drops it into the ocean where none can ever find it again."

"Just as well, Amit. Why worry? The celestial goldsmith won't send his bill to you for payment!"

"But, Lily, suppose that after millions of ages we were to meet again in the shade of the golden woods of Mars, on the shore of some vast lake. Suppose that the fisherman from *Sakuntala* were to cut open his fish, and bring out for us this wonderful, golden moment of today, and we were to be startled into recognition—what would happen then?"

"Then," said Lily, giving Amit a light stroke of her fan, "the golden moment will again be lost in the sea out of sheer absence of mind and will never be seen again. So many such moments wrought by the frenzied jeweller have been thus lost to you. You have kept no count, for you have forgotten them."

So saying, Lily hurriedly rose and joined her girl friends. A sample, this, of many such episodes in Amit's life.

"Why don't you get married, Amit?" asked his sisters Cissie and Lissie.

"The primary commodity in this business of marriage," replies Amit, "is the girl. The boy is secondary."

"You astound me," says Cissie. "As if there were a dearth of girls."

"In olden days," retorts Amit, "a girl was taken in marriage on the merit of her horoscope. I want one who needs no horoscope, who is unique, without a second on this earth."

"But when she enters your home," persists Cissie, "she'll take a second place and will be known through You."

"The girl whom in my imagination I vainly court," says Amit, "has no address. She hardly ever crosses a threshold. She flashes into my heart like a meteor from the sky and is lost in the air before she can enter a brick-and-mortar abode."

"In other words," frowns Cissie, "she's not in the least like your sisters."

"In other words," affirms Amit, "she comes not as a mere addition to the family."

"By the way, Cissie," interposes Lissie, "don't we know that Bimie Bose is only waiting for a nod from Amit to hurry to him. Now why won't he have her? Says she lacks culture !—she who stood first in M.A. with Botany ! Why, isn't learning culture?"

"Learning is the stone," says Amit, "culture is the sparkle. The one weighs, the other shines."

Lissie flares up. "Listen to him ! Bimie Bose is not good enough for him ! As though he is good enough for her ! After this I shall warn Bimie Bose never to look at Ami, even should he be crazy to marry her."

"Unless I do go crazy," retorts Amit, "why ever should I

wish to marry Bimie Bose? If ever that time comes, don't treat me with marriage but with medicine."

Amit's friends and relatives have given up all hope of his ever getting married. They are convinced that his habit of dreaming impossible dreams and shocking people by his paradoxes is only a characteristic way of evading the marital responsibility which he is incapable of shouldering. His mind is like a will-o'-the-wisp which lures and misleads in the open but which cannot be captured and brought indoors.

In the meantime Amit dashes about everywhere, entertains all sorts of acquaintances to tea at Firpo's, takes friends out for unnecessary drives at all hours of the day, buys all sorts of things at all sorts of places and gives them away indiscriminately, buys English books only to leave them behind in other houses, where they remain unclaimed.

What exasperates his sisters most in Amit is his habit of saying shocking things. In any decent gathering he is sure to say something which will scandalise everyone present.

One day he cut short a political philosopher's panegyric on democracy by remarking, "When the lifeless form of Sati was cut into pieces by Vishnu, a hundred and more holy spots sprang up, here, there, everywhere, wherever her dismembered limbs fell. Our democracy today is engaged in worshipping the like scattered fragments of a dead aristocracy. And petty aristocrats are rising up all over the earth—political aristocrats, literary aristocrats, social aristocrats. All of them vulgar, for not one of them believes in himself."

Another day when a zealous champion of feminism and social reform was engaged in a diatribe against man for his despotism over woman, Amit, removing the cigarette from his lips, interposed, "Once man's despotism is removed, woman's will begin. The despotism of the weak is terrible indeed."

All the females and the feminists present burst out scandalised. "What do you mean?"

Amit answered, "Those who have power bind the victim in chains, that is, they must first overpower. But those who have no chains drug their victim with opium, that is, they dement. The first indeed bind but they do not dement; the second bind as well as dement. Women carry opiates in their bags, and Nature's devilry keeps up the supply."

One day the subject of discussion at their Ballygunge literary gathering happened to be the poetry of Rabindranath Tagore. For the first time in his life Amit had agreed to take the chair and had gone there fully determind to give battle. The speaker was a harmless representative of the old order, endeavouring to prove that Tagore's poetry was poetry. With the exception of one or two professors, all seemed to agree that the proofs were fairly convincing. Then rose the chairman and spoke:

"A poet must poetise for no more than five years, from his twenty-fifth to his thirtieth year. From his successor we shall demand, not something better, but something different. When the mango season is over, we don't demand better mangoes; rather we demand fresh and big custard-apples. The green coconut lasts only a while—the milky flow is ephemeral; but the ripe coconut lasts ever so long—the dry kernel endures. And so the poets are ephemeral, while the philosophers are ageless. The strongest objection against Rabindranath Tagore is that this gentleman, imitating old Wordsworth, insists most perversely on continuing. Many a time the messenger of Death has called to switch off the light, but even as the old man rises from his throne, he still clings to its arms. If he doesn't quit of his own accord, it becomes our duty to quit his court in a body. The one who succeeds him will also enter in triumph, thundering and bragging that there shall be no end to his rule, that the very heavens shall be chained to the gate of his mortal abode. For a time his devotees will feed him and fete him and adore him, until the auspicious hour of the sacrifice arrives, when the devotees will clamour for liberation from the bondage of devotion. Such is the way the four-footed god is worshipped in Africa. Such is also the way the two-footed, three-footed, four-footed and fourteen-footed gods of metre may be worshipped. No desecration can compare with the

profanity of dragging out devotion till it is hackneyed....
. Admiration too has its evolution. If what we admired five years ago continues to cling to its pedestal, it is obvious that the poor thing is not aware that it no longer lives. It needs a little jolting from the outside to prove to it that the sentimental kith and kin have been delaying the burial rites too long, obviously with the intention of cheating the legitimate heirs of their rightful succession. I have sworn to expose publicly this illicit conspiracy of the Tagorites."

Our Manibhushan broke in, flashing his spectacles, "Would you then banish loyalty from literature?"

"Absolutely. The cult of literary dictatorship is fast becoming obsolete. My second contention against Rabindranath Tagore is that his literary creations are rounded or wave-like, like his handwriting, reminding one of roses and moons and female faces. Primitive, so to copy Nature's hand. From the new dictator we expect creations straight and sharp like thorns, like arrows, like spearheads. Not like flowers, but like a flash of lightning, like the pain of neuralgia—angular and piercing like a Gothic church, not rounded like a temple porch. Even if they looked like a jute-mill or a government secretariat, I wouldn't mind .... Down with the witchery of rhythmic fetters! Tear your mind away from it even as Ravana tore away Sita. If the mind protests and weeps and wails, it must still be dragged away. If the aged Jatayu rushes to intervene, let him meet his death. Before long, no doubt, the monkey-world of Kishkindhya will be roused and a Hanuman will suddenly swoop on Lanka, set the city on fire and carry the mind back to its old abode. Then shall we celebrate our reunion with Tennyson and shed streams of tears on Byron's neck and beg forgiveness of Dickens, pleading that we spurned him for a while only to cure us of our own enchantment …. If every dream-mad architect, since the time of the Mughals, had built bubbles of marble domes all over this anciet land, then every decent man would have been compelled to retire to the forest, as soon as he reached the age of twenty. To be able to appreciate the Taj Mahal one must break away from its enchantment." (It should be mentioned here that under the impact of arguments which he could not comprehend, the reporter's head was in a whirl. His report proved to be even more incomprehensible than Amit's speech. The few bits that could be salvaged have been put in order and reproduced above.)

At the reference to the Taj one of Tagore's admirers flared up with a flushed face.

"The more good things we have, the better for us."

"Quite the contrary," retorted Amit. In the order of Nature scarcity creates excellence, excess degrades it to mediocrity. Poets who are not ashamed to stick on for sixty or seventy years cheapen themselves and must suffer the consequences. In the end they are ringed round by their own imitators who make faces at them. Their writings lose all character and, pilfering from their own past, they degenerate into mere receivers of stolen property. In such cases it is incumbent on the reading public, in the interests of humanity, not to let these aged futilities linger on— I mean poetically, of course, not physically. Let them linger on as old professors, as old politicians, as old critics."

A previous speaker asked, "May we know the name of your new literary dictator?"

"Nibaran Chakravarty!" Amit readily replied.

"Nibaran Chakravarty? Who might he be?" came a chorus of surprised voices.

"Today this question is a little seed," answered Amit, "tomorrow the answer will grow to a mighty tree."

"In the meantime we would like to have a specimen."

"Then listen." Amit drew out of his pocket a long narrow canvas-bound note-book and began to read:

> *I am the Unfamiliar,*
> > *I burst upon the respectable rabble*
> > > *Like fate's ribald laughter.*
> *Shackle me with chains?*

Assail me with scriptures?
I shall blow them to bits
And freeing myself give freedom to you.
My words like a mighty fist
Shall stun the obtuse mind
And my frenzied rhythm shall confuse
The seekers of easy salvation.
They beat their brows
And one by one, in terror, in rage, in tears
Shall bow to the triumph of the Unfamiliar.[1]

The Tagorites were silenced for the day and departed, not without a threat to resume the controversy, this time in black and white.

As they drove home in Amit's car after this successful rout of his audience, Cissie remarked:

"Surely you brought this invention of yours—this Nibaran Chakravarty—ready-made in your pocket only to confound these good people."

Amit answered, "To hasten the advent of the unarrived is to act like Providence. It's Providence's part that I have

---

[1] The English rendering is a bare skeleton of the original poem which is much longer in size and is appropriately rugged and unorthodox in structure and diction.

played. This day Nibaran Chakravarty has arrived on earth. Henceforth his march will be irresistible."

Cissie is secretly very proud of her brother. She asked, "Do you sit up every morning, Amit, and fashion your stock of smart sayings for the day?"

"To be prepared for all possibilities," replied Amit, "is the way of civilization. Barbarism is always caught unawares. This too is jotted down in my note-book."

"But you seem to have no convictions whatever of your own. You always say what sounds smart at the moment."

"Were I to smear the mirror of my mind with set convictions of my own, it would no longer reflect the shadow of each fleeting moment."

"Ami, your life will be spent among shadows," said Cissie.

Collision

Amit at last decided to go to Shillong. Two reasons influenced his choice: none of his set ever went there: nor was the hunting of eligible bridegrooms so very aggressive in that quarter. The particular divine Archer who took Amit's heart for his target limited his range to the fashionable area; and of all the pleasure resorts on the hills Shillong offered the least scope for his target practice. Amit's sisters had declared their minds with a firm shake of their heads: "You may go, if you must. We shan't."

Wrapped in cloaks of imitation Persian shawl, with dainty, up-to-date parasols in their left hands and tennis rackets in their right, the sisters left for Darjeeling. Bimie Bose had already preceded them. When she saw the sisters arrive without the brother, she looked around and discovered that in Darjeeling there was a crowd but no company.

Amit had announced to everybody that he was going to Shillong to enjoy solitude. Before long, however, he discovered that the absence of a crowd somehow took the relish off the solitude. Amit had no fancy for out-dooring with the camera. He declared he was not of the tourist kind. He must taste with his mind the flavour of the sights; merely to swallow them visually was not his way.

He succeeded in whiling away a few days, reading books on the hill-slopes under the shade of the deodars. He did not touch novels, for reading novels on holidays is a practice of the Philistines. Instead he began Suniti Chatterjee's "The Origin and Development of the Bengali Language," solely in the hope of discovering a loophole for a polemic with the author. In between his fits of philology and of lassitude the hills and the mountains and the woods now and again struck him as beautiful, but the sense of beauty did not deepen and fill his mind—like the introductory phrase of a melody endlessly repeated without the theme ever reaching completion. A confused mass of scattered impressions without a sense of unity to link them up. A lack of unity in his own universe was responsible for a constant sense of restlessness and frustration in Amit, no less painful here than in town. But while in town he could beguile it away in various ways, here the restlessness seemed to settle and grow heavy on him—like an arrested waterfall imprisoned in a lake. Just as he had made up his mind to turn his back on these mountains and tramp through the plains of Sylhet and Silchar, as his mood led him, came the monsoon, and every hill and every forest was shrouded with suspended showers. It was reported that at Cherapunji the mountain ranges had effectively obstructed the onslaught of the vaporous hordes, and that very soon the waterfalls, let loose by the heavy showers, would be running riot over the mountains. Thereupon Amit decided to localise himself for a few days in the Dak Bungalow at Cherapunji and there work up a Cloud-Messenger whose heroine, unlike the heroine of Kalidasa's classic, would resemble the disembodied lightning, continually flashing across the mind's sky, without either tracing her name or leaving her address behind.

He donned his coarse woollen Highlander stockings, thick, strong-soled boots, a khaki Norfolk jacket over shorts, and a sola hat. Far from resembling Kalidasa's hero, as Abanindranath Tagore has drawn him, he looked more like a district engineer out on road repairs. However, he carried with him a few pocket editions of verse in diverse tongues.

The road leading to Amit's house was narrow and crooked, on its right a precipice overgrown with jungle. As there was little likelihood of other traffic, Amit was driving his car rather carelessly, neglecting the horn. He was fancying that since smoke, water, air and the spark which, according to the Sanskrit poet, had synthesized to form the cloud-messenger, were all present in their proper proportion in the automobile, a motor-messenger in these modern times was the right thing to send to the distant beloved; and if the driver were given a letter, no room would be left for any vagueness or mistiness. Forthwith he resolved that, on the first day of the next rainy season, he would inaugurate the modern mission of the automobile by retracing the route of its classical prototype. Who knows?—by some miracle of fate he might come upon the destined one waiting for him by the way, like one of the sonorous-named heroines of Kalidasa, an Avantika or a Malavika or one of the nymphs of the Himalayan deodars, keeping vigil for the footsteps of her lover! Just then, as he reached a curve, he suddenly saw a car coming up the opposite way. There was no room to pass. Amit pulled the brake but before it could work the other car came up against his. There was a collision—but no catastrophe. The other car jerked back a little and came to rest against the mountain side.

A maiden stepped out of the car and halted. Against the somber background of imminent death she flashed like a figure etched by lightning—luminously isolated from the surrounding gloom. Amit saw a rare vision, as though a Lakshmi had risen from the ocean which the gods had churned and stood poised above the foaming and raging waters. Had Amit seen this same girl in a city drawing-room, in the midst of half a dozen others, he might have noticed her but would have missed this revelation of the full splendour of her being. May be there are persons in this world who are worth looking at, but one rarely sees them in the right setting.

She was dressed in white sari of a fine woollen fabric, narrow bordered, with jacket to match, and wore white leather shoes of Indian pattern. A tall slim figure, complexion of lustrous brown, dark long-drawn eyes full of deep repose under thick lashes, an open forehead from which the hair had been drawn back and tied, thus freely exposing the rounded loveliness of a face like a fruit about to ripen. The sleeves of her jacket reached her wrists, where they met two plain and solitary bangles. The loose shoulder-end of her sari, unhampered by a brooch, was lifted over her head, where it had been fastened to the hair by a silver pin of Cuttack workmanship.

Leaving his hat inside the car, Amit came and stood before her, speechless like one awaiting chastisement. The maiden seemed touched by this pose of helplessness and not a little amused. At last Amit managed to mumble, "I'm sorry, I bungled."

She laughed. "No bungling. Just a mishap—and I began it."

The girl's voice had the rounded cadence of a fountain's

overflow, broad and smooth like the voice of a young boy. When Amit returned home that evening he spent a long time racking his brain for an image that would aptly describe the quality of her voice—a voice that seemed to have a flavour, a touch of its own. At last he opened his Notebook and jotted: "Her voice floats like the delicate fumes of scented tobacco in the hookah, mellowed by their passage through water, cured of the acrid taste of nicotine and touched with the subtle aroma of the rose."

By way of apology the girl added, "I was going to meet a friend who, I was told, had arrived. We had hardly gone up a little when the chauffeur said that we had come the wrong way. As there was no room to turn the car, we were going ahead, when your car crashed into ours from above."

"There's something above even the car from above," said Amit. "The ugly malicious star whose mischief is the cause of it all."

At this juncture the chauffeur reported that, though the car had not been seriously damaged, it would take some time to get it into running order.

"If you'll pardon this guilty automobile of mine," ventured Amit, "I'll be only too happy to take you wherever you wish to go."

"Thanks. It's hardly necessary. I'm used to walking on these mountain paths."

"The necessity is mine—a proof of your forgiveness."

The girl hesitated a little and remained silent. Amit went on, "There's just one thing more. Driving a car is no great merit and one can't drive on to posterity; still I consider myself unfortunate that your very first knowledge of me should be to my discredit. Please allow me to prove that my worth in this world is at least equal to your driver's."

For fear of unknown dangers girls are shy of their first introduction to strangers. But the shock of the accident had to a large extent broken down the preliminary barrier. Fate in its impatience suddenly halted them in the middle of the lonely mountain road to link their minds in a mutual revelation. The vision revealed by the sudden lightning flash would continue to flit across the screen of darkness to haunt the wakeful eye. Its deep impress was etched on the very centre of their consciousness as the fiery blaze of the solar system was etched on the blue sky in the shock of a gigantic cosmic upheaval.

Without further protest the girl took her seat in the car. She gave directions and when the car reached its destination, she got out and said, "If you can spare the time, please drop in here tomorrow. I should like to introduce you to the lady of the house."

Amit felt like saying. "I can come right away. I have enough time." But a feeling of embarrassment sealed his lips.

Returning home he jotted down in his Notebook: "What madness was this of the road! To have torn two individuals from two different spots and set them going—maybe from this day onwards—on one and the same path! The astronomers are mistaken. It was from an unknown sphere that the moon rushed into the earth's orbit—their cars collided and ever since that fatal shock the two have run their course in common, age after age, the light of each shining on the face of the other. Their union in motion has never been severed. Deep within me I hear my heart attest that we, too, have begun our march hand in hand, picking up luminous instants on the way and threading them into the garland of our journey. No more for us the waiting at fortune's door for our fixed allowance and our fixed wages. Henceforth all our dealings shall be sudden and momentous."

It was raining. Striding up and down the veranda. Amit burst into a silent invocation: "Where are you, Nibaran Chakravarty! Come now to my aid, give me words, give me voice!" Out came the thin, long note book and Nibaran Chakravarty dictated a poem.

Retrospect

The first phase of the introduction of English education into Bengal was marked by a series of disturbances in the social weather, generated by the uneven distribution of atmospheric pressure between the old seats of learning and the new schools and colleges. Gianadashankar had been caught in this storm. He belonged by birth to the old generation but had been suddenly blown far ahead into the new. Born before his time, neither in outlook, nor in speech, nor in habits did he contemporise with his contemporaries. Like the sea-bird that loves to rock on the wave, he loved to bare his breast to the blast of social calumny.

When the progeny of such a grandfather take upon

themselves to set right the freaks of the calendar, they usually head straight for the opposite terminus. Which is what happened to Gianadashankar's grandson, Varadashankar. This gentleman, after his father's death, contrived to become anachronously the remote ancestor of his immediate progenitors. He was a devotee of the Serpent-goddess and supplicated the Goddess of Smallpox as mother; drank water amulet-charmed and spent the morning writing out the one thousand names of the goddess Durga. All his life he waged war against the pretensions of non-Brahmins to knowledge, and with the help of Pandits of unimpeachable orthodoxy he published innumerable pamphlets to save Hinduism from the contamination of science, sparing no expense in flinging gratuitously at the heads of the new intelligentsia the hoary wisdom of the sages. Within a short time, by his indefatigable observance of prescribed piety, ritual and penance, he fortified and made impregnable the fortress of immovable orthodoxy.

When at the age of twenty-seven he gave up the ghost he carried with him to the other world the blessings of innumerable Brahmins, on whom he had showered, in the name of father, mother and daughter, gifts of cows, gold, and land.

Varada's wife Yogamaya was the daughter of his father's intimate friend Ramlochan Banerjee. They had been college chums and had frequented the same hotels and shared the forbidden dishes of foreign chops and cutlets. At the time of the marriage there had been no conflict between the ways of the two households, her father's and her father-in-law's. The girls in their father's house were educated and were wont to move about freely; some of them even wrote of their travels in the illustrated monthlies. After the death of her father-in-law her husband set himself to the task of effecting a thorough-going reformation in her culture. Yogamaya's movements were severely restricted under various passport regulations drawn up in accordance with the imperative requirements of the traditional policy of frontier protection. Over her eyes descended the veil, and on her mind too. Even the person of the goddess of learning was subjected to a thorough search before she could obtain the necessary permit to enter the zenana. English books in her possession were forthwith forfeited and among the Bengali books only the pre-Bankim literature had any chance of being permitted to cross the threshold. A Bengali translation of *Yoga-Vashistha Ramayana* in deluxe binding had long adorned Yogamaya's bookshelf. Till the last day of his mortal tenure the master of the house had earnestly hoped that she would one day find time by way of recreation to study this classic of spiritual discourses.

Hard as it was for Yogamaya to fold herself up as a safe deposit in the steel chest of the Puranas, she had learnt to bridle her rebellious mind. Her refuge from this mental confinement was their family priest Pandit Dinasharan

Vedantaratna, who greatly appreciated her natural and bright intelligence. He frankly told her: "This rigmarole of rite and ritual is not for such as you, my daughter. The foolish not only cheat themselves but are cheated by the whole world as well. Do you imagine that we ourselves believe in all this? Haven't you noticed how we turn and twist the Shastras, without any compunction, to suit our convenience? It only means that we have little faith in these observances. We play the fool to please the fool. But since you don't want to cheat yourself, I shall be the last person to deceive you. You send for me at your pleasure and I shall read out to you such portions of the scriptures as I believe to be true."

Now and then he came and read out and expounded for Yogamaya passages from the *Gita* or the *Brahmabhashya*. She asked such intelligent questions that the Pandit was delighted and his enthusiasm in discussing them with her knew no bounds. The Pandit had little respect for the menagerie of spiritual instructors Varadashankar had collected round him. He confessed to Yogamaya that she was the only one in the whole town with whom he found it a pleasure to discourse. "You have saved me from self-contempt, my daughter," he said. Thus ringed round by an incessant succession of fasts and rites, Yogamaya, ordinance-bound (to borrow a phrase from our journalists' jargon), managed to survive this scripture-shackled phase of life.

After her husband's death, however, she led her own life with her son Jatishankar and her daughter Surama, spending the winter in Calcutta, the summer at one of the hill resorts. Jatishankar was in college, but for Surama, failing to find a girls' school that suited her taste, she secured after considerable difficulty the services of a private tutor, Labanyalata. It was this lady whom Amit had met so suddenly, this morning.

Labanya's Past

Labanya's father, Abanish Dutta, was principal of a college in western India. He had looked after his motherless daughter so well that not even the constant grinding at university exminations had damaged her intellectual development. Indeed, remarkable as it may seem, her love of study survived her academic career.

Learning was her father's only passion and in his daughter that passion had found its perfect fulfilment. Hence he loved his daughter even more than he loved his library. It was his belief that a person whose mind had been properly baked by knowledge need never marry, since all the possible apertures through which the gas of random fancies might find its way would have been sealed. He firmly believed that whatever soft ground might have remained in his daughter's mind for the tender passions had been finally paved and cemented with concrete facts of history and mathematics, so that nothing from outside could now make the slightest impression. He had even considered the possibility of her never marrying. "What if she did not marry! Let her be wedded to knowledge!"

Sobhanlal was another object of his affection. It was rare to find a boy of his age so devoted to learning. His broad forehead, the transparent frankness in his eyes, the genial curve of his lips, the candid smile on his youthful, handsome face attracted all who saw him. He was, however, extremely shy and was overcome by nervous confusion if the slightest attention was paid to him.

He came of a poor family and had been laboriously climbing the academic ladder on the rungs of free scholarships. His professor took no small pride in the anticipation that Sobhanlal would one day become famous and that he himself would have the credit of having been the chief architect of his fame. Sobhan used to come to him for guidance and had unrestricted access to his library. The sight of Labanya used to fill him with confusion. His shrinking, retreating shyness cut a poor figure in the eyes of Labanya with the result that he was relegated to the usual fate of hesitant males who lack the courage to convince the other sex of their existence.

All of a sudden one day Sobhanlal's father Nanigopal invaded Abanish's house and subjected the professor to a volley of abuse. He alleged that the professor had laid a trap in his house and was luring marriageable boys into it, on the pretext of teaching them. He charged him with the sinister intent to decaste a high-caste boy like Sobhan for the luxury of indulging his whim of social reform. By way of evidence he exhibited a pencil-sketch of Labanya which, he alleged, had been discovered inside his son's trunk, overlaid with rose petals. Nanigopal had no doubt that it was a souvenir from Labanya. His calculating brain had already made an exact estimate of Sobhanlal's current value in the marriage market as also of its probable rise if the commodity were held back a little while longer. Abanish's designs for capturing such a valuable possession gratis seemed to him little short of burglary with housebreaking. It was as good as stealing cash.

Until then Labanya had been totally unaware of the existence of a secret altar where, screened from sceptical eyes, her image was being regularly worshipped. In a corner of Abanish's library, buried under a jumble of discarded pamphlets and magazines, Sobhanlal had fortuitously come across a faded, uncared-for photograph of Labanya. He had a copy made by an artist friend and had returned the original to the old place. The roses too were from his friend's garden and were as naturally grown and as innocent of all suggestion of unseemly impertinence as was his own bashful and secret love. Nevertheless he had to take the punishment. With bent head and flushed cheeks, wiping a secret tear, the shy youth bade farewell to the house.

From a distance Sobhanlal gave a final proof of his dedicated love of which none knew save He who knows the secrets of all men's hearts. In the B.A. examination he had topped the list while Labanya had stood third. This fact had greatly humiliated and pained Labanya—for two reasons. Her father's immense admiration for Sobhan's intellect had long hurt her vanity, while the knowledge that this admiration was not unmixed with affection had but served to aggravate the sense of mortification. She had striven her utmost to get the better of him in the academic contests, but when she found that he had outstripped her, she found it hard to forgive him. The suspicion rankled in her mind that this disparity in the examination results was due to the special attention her father had given to Sobhanlal, though the boy had never approached Abanish for tutorial coaching. For a good many days after, Labanya would turn her face away and walk out at Sobhanlal's approach. In the M. A. examination too, Labanya stood no chance of scoring a triumph over Sobhanlal. And yet she did. Even Abanish was surprised. Had Sobhanlal been a poet he would have filled a volume with verses; instead he presented her with a fat lot of examination marks by the simple process of renouncing his claim to them.

Their academic career was now over. Soon after, Abanish had the extremely painful experience of suddenly realizing in his own person that, howsoever tightly the mind is stuffed full of learning, there always remains some cranny which Cupid can sneak into. He was then forty-seven, at which extremely vulnerable age a widow, scaling the rampart of his scholarship, cutting through the solid phalanx of tomes in his library, stole straight into his heart. There was nothing to stand in the way of his marriage save his love for Labanya, between which and his new passion a fierce conflict ensued. He sat down to study with great zeal, but even more zealous proved the mind's obsession with lovely fancies. Books for review, his favourite books on Buddhist archeology, came to him from the office of the *Modern Review,* and there they lay before him unopened, while he sat motionless like some Buddhist stupa burdened with the silence of centuries. The editor, would begin to lose patience, but such is inevitably the fate of a savant's stupa of wisdom, once it is shaken. What can save an elephant that has stepped on quicksands?

A belated sense of remorse now haunted Abanish. It occurred to him that may be, hypnotised as he had been by books, he had not had the time to notice that his daughter loved Sobhanlal, for not to fall in love with a boy like Sobhanlal would have been too unnatural of her. He was disgusted with fathers in general and with himself and Nanigopal in particular.

About this time there came a letter from Sobhanlal, asking if the professor could lend him a few books from his library to help him in his thesis on the Gupta Dynasty which he was preparing for the Premchand Roychand Scholarship. Forthwith Abanish wrote back a warm reply inviting him to come and make a free use of his library, as he had been wont to do in the earlier days.

A flutter seized Sobhanlal's heart. He took it for granted that at the back of this enthusiastic letter lay perhaps the tacit approval of Labanya. He began to frequent the library. Passing in and out of the hall he now and again caught a fleeting glimpse of Labanya, when he would deliberately slacken his pace, in the fond hope that she would exchange a word with him, ask him how he was, evince some interest in the subject he was working on. How he would have loved to discuss it with her and show her his notes, had she but asked! He was particularly eager to know what Labanya thought of some of his theories on the subject. But so far not a word had been exchanged; nor had he the courage to venture without encouragement.

Some days passed. It was a Sunday. Sobhanlal had just arranged his papers on the table and was turning over the pages of a book, occasionally taking notes. It was midday and there was no one else in the room. Taking advantage of the holiday, Abanish had gone out to pay a visit. He had not named the house; he only left word that they were not to expect him to tea.

Suddenly the door flew open. Sobhanlal's heart began to thump. Labanya entered. Sobhanlal rose from his seat, overcome with confusion, altogether at a loss what to do. Fierce as a flame, Labanya hissed, "Why do you come to this house?"

Sobhanlal gave a violent start. No word came from his lips.

"Do you know what your father said about your coming here? Aren't you ashamed of humiliating me?"

With downcast eyes Sobhanlal mumbled, "Please forgive me. I will leave at once."

He could not even explain that her own father had invited him to the house. He gathered up his papers. His hands were trembling violently, a dumb pain beat against his ribs seeking an outlet in vain. Crestfallen he made his exit from the house.

When an impediment crosses the way of love and we are prevented from loving someone whom we might have loved, then such a person becomes for us an object, not of indifference, but of the very opposite of love, blind hatred. Perhaps, unknown even to herself, Labanya had once waited to shower her gift of love on Sobhanlal. But Sobhanlal had failed to make the right overture. Since then everything had gone against him—this last incident the unkindest cut of all. In the bitterness of her mortification Labanya had grievously misjudged her father; she imagined that he had purposefully invited Sobhanlal to court her, hoping thereby to get rid of her and obtain freedom for himself. Hence the magnitude of her wrath against the innocent youth.

Thereafter Labanya by her own stubborn insistence brought about the marriage of her father. Abanish had set aside half his savings for his daughter. After his marriage, however, Labanya declared that she would not touch a farthing of her father's money and announced her intention of earning her own living. Abanish was deeply hurt. "I did not want this marriage," he protested. "It was you, Labanya, who insisted on it. Why then must you boycott me in this fashion?"

Labanya replied, "I am doing it to prevent our relationship from being spoilt. Don't you worry, father. Let me be happy in my own way. All I want is your blessings."

She got a job and took sole charge of Surama's studies. She could easily have taken charge of Jati's studies as well, but he flatly refused to submit to the indignity of being taught by a woman.

Life passed tolerably smoothly, regulated by the daily routine. Her spare hours were devoted to the reading of English literature from early times to the age of Bernard Shaw and in particular to the study of Greek and Roman history with the help of Grote, Gibbon and Gilbert

Murray. Not that no breath of disquiet ever ruffled the placidity of her mind, but there was little room in her life for the passage of a more solid mischief. And now, right in the middle of the road, the mischief overtook her in a car, without even a warning sound. All of a sudden Greek and Roman history lost its gigantic weight. One intense moment of the immediate present, brushing all else aside, shook her and said, Awake! In a moment Labanya was awake. At long last she was aware of herself. Not learning but pain brought her the awareness.

Aquaintance

From the ruins of the past let us now revert to the present.

Labanya asked Amit to wait in the study and went to inform Yogamaya. Amit sat in the room as a bee sits inside a lotus. Whichever way he turned he was aware of a subtle presence which filled his mind with a delicious ecstasy. On the shelf and on the desk he noticed English books of literary taste. They all seemed to vibrate with life. They were Labanya's books, read by her; her fingers had turned their pages, her thoughts had hovered over them day and night, her eager eyes had traced their lines, her lap had been their resting place in her moods of listlessness. He started when he caught sight of a volume of Donne's

Poetical Works on the table. In Oxford the poetry of Donne and his contemporaries had been the main subject of his critical study. Now, by happy chance, this poetry had proved to be a meeting place where their minds seemed to touch each other.

The prolonged wear of uninspired days and nights had rendered Amit's existence drab and colourless, like a textbook in the hands of a school-master, used year after year till its cover is ready to fall off. The morrow inspired no lively curiosity, nor was there any reason for him to welcome with open arms each day as it came. But now in a moment he felt transported to an altogether new planet. Here matter weighed less, the feet seemed to float above earth, each moment was an impatient lure to the inconceivable, the body felt the caress of the breeze and longed to be a flute, the light of the sky passed into the blood, its accumulated warmth like sap that surges up every limb of a tree, filled with the ecstasy of flowers. The dust-laden veil that had lain over the mind so long was blown away, and the uncommon peeped through the commonplace. And so when Yogamaya slowly entered the room, this very simple event struck Amit with wonder. "This is not a mere entrance," he exclaimed within himself, "it is an advent."

Yogamaya was about forty. The years had added dignity but no flabbiness to her limbs. Fair-skinned, her complexion was radiant, the hair cropped close as is the custom with Hindu widows, her eyes filled with the peace of motherly devotion, her smile gentle and calm, her figure draped in coarse white cotton, the head covered. Her immaculate, beautiful feet were bare. As Amit touched them in respectful greeting, he felt the benediction of a goddess thrill through his veins.

The introductions over, Yogamaya said, "Your uncle Amaresh was the best lawyer in our district. Once when we were almost ruined by a devastating suit, he came to our rescue. He used to call me Boudidi."[1]

"I am his unworthy nephew," said Amit. "My uncle saved you from loss, I have put you to some. You were his Boudidi in gain, you will be my Mashima[2] in loss."

Yogamaya asked: "Is your mother living?"

"She once was. I should have had an aunt as well."

"Why this aunt-sickness, my son?"

"Think, if I had smashed my mother's car today, she would never have ceased to chide me for what she would have called my monkeying. But if the car is Mashima's she merely smiles at my clumsiness and dismisses it as a childish prank."

---

1. A term of address for the elder brother's wife.
2. Auntie.

Yogamaya smiled, "Well, then, let the car be Mashima's."

Springing to his feet Amit touched Yogamaya's feet and said, "That is why one must believe in the fruit of past karma. I was blest with a mother and so did no penance to obtain a Mashima. Smashing a car can hardly be described as a good karma, and yet in a trice a Mashima appears in my life like a boon from the gods. Think, what ages of preparation must lie behind this miracle."

Yogamaya smiled. "The fruit of whose karma?—yours, mine or the garage mechanic's?"

Passing his fingers through his thick crop of hair Amit answered, "A hard question indeed. Not one individual's karma. The entire universe from star to star, from age to age, had conspired to work this convulsion, timed exactly at forty-eight minutes past nine of this Friday. And then?"

Darting a side-long glance at Labanya, Yogamaya smiled. Without waiting to know Amit better she made up her mind that these two must marry. To this end she said, "While you two entertain yourselves, let me hasten to make arrangements for lunch."

Amit had the gift of the gab. He immediately began, "Mashima has ordered us to get acquainted. At the very beginning of acquaintance comes the name. Let the names then be determined first of all. I suppose you know my name, that is, what in English is called the proper name."

"All that I know," said Labanya, "is that your name is Amit Babu."

"Not in all cases."

Labanya smiled. "Cases may be many but the name should be one."

"What you suggest is hardly up-to-date. Men, nations and ages, they all vary. To say that the name alone does not vary is unscientific. I have decided to make myself famous by my advocacy of the relativity of names. But at the very outset I must inform you that on your lips my name shall not be Amit Babu."

"May be you prefer the English way—Mister Roy."
"Altogether a distant name imported from overseas. To measure the efficacy of a name we must see how long the sound takes to travel from the ear to the heart."

"Let's hear the fleet-footed name."

"To increase the speed one must lighten the weight. Cut out Babu from Amit Babu."

"Not so easy. Takes time."

"Not for all. There is no such thing as the watch in this universe. The pocket watch varies from pocket to pocket. That's Einstein's theory."

Labanya got up. "The water for your bath is getting cold." she said.

"I'll willingly put up with a cold bath if you'll only stay and talk a while longer."

"I'm sorry. I've no time. I must get busy." Saying so Labanya left the room.

Amit did not immediately go to bathe. He sat on and mused, trying to recall how each smiling word formed itself between her lips. Amit had met many beautiful girls; their beauty was like the full-moon night, bright yet obscure. But Labanya's beauty was like the early morning; there was no lure of mystery about it, it was radiant with the light of intelligence. At the time of her creation Providence must have put something masculine into her make-up. One had only to see her to know that she had the power not only of feeling but of thought as well. Which is what fascinated Amit so much. Amit himself had intellect but no forbearance, judgment but no patience; he had read much and learnt much but of tranquillity he had achieved nothing. In Labanya's face he saw a picture of serenity, born not of emotional self-complacency but of the profound poise of a calm and balanced mind.

6

Intimacy

Amit was by nature social. He could not for long be content with nature's beauty. He needed to talk. He was used to it. One cannot play the wag with trees and mountains. If one played pranks with them, one only invited physical rebuffs. They live by law and expect others to abide by law. In a word, they have no sense of humour. And so Amit had felt like a fish out of water whenever he strayed outside a city. But now a strange thing happened. The Shilling hills seemed to fill his being with their rapture. Today he rose before the sun—a habit quite contrary to his nature. Looking through the window he saw that the sun, from beyond the hills, had already drawn with his brush long, golden strokes on the thin layer of clouds behind the trembling fringe of the deodars. He could not but gaze in silence at the play of colours touched with fire.

Gulping down a cup of tea Amit left the house. The road was deserted. Underneath an ancient moss-grown pine he found a seat on the thick carpet of its fragrant needles. He stretched his legs and lighted a cigarette which he held unmindfully between his fingers without smoking. The forest lay on the way to Yogamaya's house. Just as, before sitting down to a meal, one relishes the smell from the kitchen, so Amit inhaled the glory of Yogamaya's house from this spot. He waited for his watch to announce the right hour when he could go over and claim a cup of tea. At first his visits had been restricted to evenings. Amit's reputation for literary taste had got him this standing invitation. On the first two or three occasions Yogamaya too had shown some enthusiasm for these literary discussions, but she soon understood that thereby she was only putting a damper on the enthusiasm of the other party. It was not difficult to understand that three is a crowd where two is company. Since then excuses for her absence began to multiply—clearly not by necessity, nor by accident, but by design. The mistress of the house had sensed beneath the literary devotion of these two a deeper devotion. Amit too understood that, despite the lady's years, her eye was sharp—though the heart was tender. His enthusiasm for the *tete-a-tete* waxed. In order to prolong the scheduled hour he offered to coach Jatishankar in his study of English literature for an hour every morning and two hours every evening. He plunged into his task with such extravagant zeal that invariably the morning lengthened into noon and the coaching into idle talk till politeness obliged him to accept Yogamaya's invitation to lunch. Thus it came about that social obligation widened its scope from hour to hour.

His coaching engagement was at eight in the morning. Normally it would have been an unearthly hour for him. He used to say that the creature whose habitation in the womb lasts ten months should not adapt his sleeping hours to the measure of birds and beasts. Till now his nights had encroached on his mornings. The stolen hours, he used to say, were so sweet because they were forbidden. But nowadays his sleep was no longer undisturbed, fretted as it was by his impatience to rise early. He woke up before he need have and dared not remain in bed lest he be late. Sometimes he even pushed the hand of his watch forward, but the fear of being found out made such repeated time-stealing impossible. Today he looked at his watch and found that the hour was still on the wrong side of seven. Surely the watch had stopped? He put it to his ear and heard it ticking.

Even as he did so he was startled by the sight of Labanya coming down the road, swinging an umbrella in her right hand. She was clad in a white sari, a black shawl with a fringed border, folded triangle-wise, thrown over her shoulders. Amit knew that Labanya had half seen him but was not disposed to acknowledge the fact in a full glance of recognition. When she reached the turning, Amit could no longer restrain himself and ran up to her.

"Well you knew you couldn't evade me, and yet you made me run. Distance is embarrassing, you know."

"How?"

"The unfortunate one lagging behind longs to shout with all his heart. But how is he to shout—what to call? One good thing about the deities is that one pleases them by invoking their names. By bawling out, Durga, Durga, one doesn't displease the ten-armed goddess. With your kind it's different."

"You might just as well refrain from calling."

"Which is only possible if you are near enough. Hence I say don't go away. What could be more tragic than that I should long to call you and yet not be able to call!"

"Why? I thought you were used to English ways."

"Miss Dutt? That might do at the tea-table. But just see, when this earth and this sky met in the first light of the dawn this morning, the intimacy of their union was celebrated in a glory which sums up both heaven and earth. Don't you hear a call resounding from earth to heaven, and from heaven to earth? Can't such a moment, creative of a name, occur in the life of us mortals? Just imagine that I have this moment called out to you, with all my soul, with all my breath. This call echoes from forest to forest and reaches that many-hued cloud in the sky. The cloud-capped mountain yonder listens and broods. Can you imagine that name to be Miss Dutt?"

"Christening takes time," said Labanya, evading the topic, "meanwhile let me finish my walk."

"It takes long to learn to walk." went on Amit, keeping at her side. "But with me it has been the other way about. It's only now after coming here, so late in life that I have learned to sit. There's a saying in English that the rolling stone gathers no moss. With that in mind I came and sat here by the wayside while it was yet dark. And so I could see the light of dawn."

"Do you know the name of that bird with green feathers?" asked Labanya, changing the conversation.

"That there are birds in this world" replied Amit, "was only a commonplace fact to me until now. I had never had occasion to feel its special significance. A miracle has happened since I came here—I have really known that there are birds, and what is more, that they sing."

"How wonderful!" laughed Labanya.

"You're laughing!" complained Amit. "Even when I am

serious, my words don't sound serious. That's the curse of mannerism. The moon was the presiding planet at my birth, and even on the most dismally moonless night she must need give at least a flicker of a smile before fading away."

"Please don't blame me," said Labanya, "even the bird would laugh, if it heard you talk."

Amit went on: "You see, people laugh at my words because they don't at first catch their meaning. If they did, they would pause and think. My saying that today I have discovered birds anew makes others laugh. And yet the underlying fact is that today I have discovered everything anew, even myself. One cannot laugh at such a fact. There you are! You yourself are now silent, though my words are almost the same."

Labanya laughed. "You are not very ancient yourself—rather too new. Why then this fancy for the still more new?"

"The answer is a profound truth which I dare not utter at the tea-table," said Amit. "What appears as new in me is the immemorial ancient—ancient like the light of dawn, like this new-born lily, ageless but discovered ever anew."

Labanya smiled and remained silent.

"This smile of yours," resumed Amit, "is like the light of

the policeman's dark lantern on a burglar. I know that you recognise what I said just now as stolen from the poet whom you admire so greatly. But please, for heaven's sake, don't thereby put me down as a confirmed plagiarist. There are times when one's self is transformed into a Sankaracharya and affirms that the difference between 'I wrote it' and 'he wrote it', is but *maya*. Why, sitting here this morning I said to myself, let me pick out a line from all the literatures known to me such as I alone could have written—this very moment. No other poet could possibly have written it."

"And could you pick one out?"

"Indeed, I did."

Labanya could not restrain her curiosity.

"What was it?"

"For God's sake hold your tongue and let me love!"

A tremor shook Labanya's heart. After a long pause Amit asked, "You know who wrote it, of course?"

Labanya inclined her head a little to indicate that she did. Amit went on.

"The other day I discovered a copy of Donne on your table, else this line could hardly have occurred to me."

"You discovered?"

"What else? Books are seen in book stalls but are revealed only on your table. The tables I have seen in public libraries only carry books, but yours I found sheltering them. No wonder Donne's poem shook my heart the other day. Other poets collect crowds at their doors, like the feeding of beggars at a rich man's funeral; but in the solitary chamber of Donne's poems there's room only for a couple to sit side by side, close to one another. No wonder I could hear so very clearly the morning's soliloquy of my heart.

For God's sake hold your tongue and let me love!"

Amit rendered the verse into Bengali. Labanya was surprised.

"Do you write verse in Bengali?"

"I am afraid I shall begin writing from now on. What havoc the new Amit Roy will perpetrate the old Amit Roy has no means of knowing. Maybe he will forthwith march out to battle."

"Battle? With whom?"

"That I can't make out. Only I feel that now, immediately I must blindly hazard my life for something magnificent. If later on I have to repent, there'll be time enough for that."

Labanya laughed. "If you need must fling away your life, fling it with care."

"The warning is unnecessary. I have no mind to rush into a communal riot. I shall take care to avoid both the Mussalman and the Britisher. But if I run across an old decrepit fogey, looking non-violently religious, blowing his horn as he drives along, I'll step in his way and shout. To battle! You know the dyspeptic sort who, instead of going into hospital, flock to the hills and shamelessly saunter about to increase their appetite."

"What if the fellow ignores you and passes by?" asked Labanya, laughing.

"Then I shall raise both my hands heavenwards and exclaim: 'This time I forgive you. You are my brother, we are children of the same Mother India.' You know, when the heart expands and becomes very big, one both fights and forgives."

Labanya laughed.

"When you proposed battle," she said, "I was frightened, but the way you have propounded your gospel of forgiveness assures me there's no cause for anxiety."

Amit asked. "Will you agree to a request of mine?"

"What is it?"

"Don't walk any more today to increase your appetite."

"Very well. What else?"

"Come, let's sit under that tree, down by that little laughing stream, under that stone with its many coloured mosses."

Labanya looked at her wrist watch.

"But there's very little time," she objected.

"That, Labanya Devi, is life's most baffling and tragic problem. If there's only half a jarful of water to last through the desert, one must see to it that the water does not spill over on the way and is lost in the sand. Punctuality befits those who have time to spare. The gods command unlimited time and that's why the sun rises in time and sets in time. Our resources are limited. For us to waste time in punctuality would be extravagance. If an immortal were to ask me, "What did you accomplish on earth?" must I shamefacedly answer, 'I was always working with my eyes on the hands of the clock, I had no time to lift them to the things beyond all time.' That's why I have to plead, come with me over there."

That another could object to what he himself approved was a possibility which Amit could not for a moment consider. This made it difficult for others to offer objection.

"Very well," Labanya yielded.

From a deep woodland glade a narrow path led downwards to a Khasi village. Ignoring its public utility, a tiny stream from a waterfall had run right across it and gone its own way, leaving behind pebbles as marks of its right of way. At that spot the two of them seated themselves on a stone, by the side of a deep hollow where the water had collected—like a purdah lady behind a green veil, afraid to step out. The very veil of solitude that hung over the place made Labanya blush with shyness as though she herself had been unveiled. She wanted to say something, anything, to hide her embarrassment, but no words came to her. She felt choked as one does in a nightmare.

Amit realized that the silence must be broken. He said, "You know there are two styles in our language, the literary and the colloquial. But besides these two we should have had a third, a speech not for society, nor for business, but for the intimacy of solitude such as this. Like the song of the birds, the music of the poets, it should have flowed from our throats as freely as a child's sobbing. It's a great shame that for lack of such expression we should have to run to bookstalls. Just imagine what would have happened if each time we wanted to laugh we had to run to the dentist's clinic. Tell me the truth, Labanya Devi, don't you feel like talking in melody now?"

Labanya bent her head and remained silent. Amit went

on. "In the speech of the tea-table one must discriminate endlessly between what is good form and what is not. But here there is neither the decent nor the indecent. What then is one to do? To put the mind at ease, one must recite a poem. Prose takes too long—we haven't the time for it. If you permit me, I shall begin."

The permission had to be given. To demur out of shyness would only expose her shame. By way of preface Amit began, "It seems you like Rabindranath's poems."

"I do."

"I don't. Wherefore please forgive me. I have my own special poet, whose compositions are so excellent that very few ever read them. Indeed, hardly any one ever honours him even with abuse. I want to recite something of his."

"Why are you so nervous about it?"

"In this respect my experience has been painful. If one runs down your celebrated poet, you outcast him; even if you merely ignore him in silence and pass by, you invite on your head a shower of harsh epithets. What I like, another may not—hence all the bloodshed, on this earth."

"You needn't fear bloodshed from me. I don't canvass another's taste to second my own."

"That's well said. Let me then begin undaunted.

O Unknown, how will you loosen my grasp
Ere I have known you?

Mark the subject! The bondage of not-knowing. The worst bondage of all. I am a prisoner in a world which is not known to me; when I know it, I shall have obtained my freedom. This is what is known as the doctrine of Mukti.

In a blind moment,
In an awakening wrapped round with slumber,
When the night was dissolving into dawn
I saw your face,
My eyes fastened on yours I asked where you lay hid,
In what secret nook of self-forgetfulness.

No cave is so dark as that wherein one loses oneself. All the treasures we have missed in life are jumbled together in this limbo of self-forgetfulness. That, however, does not justify our giving up in despair.

The knowledge of you
Will not come easily,
Not by sweet words whispered in the ear.
Victory shall be mine
Over your doubt-choked speech;
In proud strength I will lift you
Out of doubt, out of shame,

Out of the strife of misgiving,
Into the pitiless light.

Absolutely relentlessly mastered. What great strength! Mark the manly vigour of the composition.

Bathed in tears you shall awake
And know yourself in a trice.
The bond shall break,
In giving you freedom I shall find my own.

No such strain will you find in that celebrated writer of yours. This is like a tempest of fire in the solar system. This is not a mere lyric, it's the hard, pitiless core of life.

Fixing his gaze on Labanya, Amit went on.

"O Unknown,
The day is spent, the dusk descends, time will not wait;
In one sharp sudden swoop
Let the flame of the knowledge of you burn high and bright,
And let my life be poured into it as an offering!"

Before the recitation was over, Amit had caught hold of Labanya's hand. She did not resist. She looked into his face and said no word. No words were necessary. Labanya forgot to look at her watch.

Matchmaking

Amit went up to Yogamaya and said, "Mashima, I've come on a matchmaker's mission. Please do not dismiss me in niggardly fashion."

"Provided I approve. First out with the name, address and description."

"The name is no measure of the candidate's worth."

"In that case, I am afraid, the match-maker will have to forfeit a portion of his fee."

"That's unfair. The world of those with big names is spacious outside but narrow at home. Their time is spent in maintaining the grandeur of their life rather than its happiness. Such men can spare only a fraction of themselves for their wives, not at all enough for a proper marriage. A big man's marriage is a partial marriage, as reprehensible as polygamy."

"Very well, let's take the name for granted. What about his looks?"

"I am loath to comment, for fear of exaggerating."

"Exaggeration, I suppose, is the trick of your trade."

"In choosing a bridegroom two things need to be considered—his name must not outgrow the home nor his looks outstrip the wife's."

"All right, never mind the name and looks. What of the rest?"

"What remains is collectively known as worth. The fellow is not worthless."

"Brains?"

"Enough to outwit others into believing that he has enough."

"Learning?"

"Even like Newton's. He knows that he is merely gathering pebbles on the seashore of knowledge. Unlike Newton, he dare not say so in public, lest people take him at his word."

"The list of the bridegroom's qualifications seems a modest one."

"To advertise Annapurna's plenitude Siva agrees to call himself a beggar, nor is he in the least ashamed of it."

"It that case let the introduction be a little more explicit."

"Known family. Prospective bridegroom's name Amit Roy. Why do you laugh, Mashima? Do you think the proposal a joke?"

"I confess, my boy, I am afraid lest the whole thing turn out to be a joke in the end."

"Such a suspicion casts a reflection on the boy."

"It's no small achievement to be able to keep one's world light with laughter."

"The gods, Mashima, wield that power. Which is why they are not fit to be bridegrooms. Damayanti knew that well."

"Do you really like my Labanya?"

"What test would you suggest?"

"In the certitude that she is yours lies your only test."

"Please explain yourself more fully."

"I shall recognise a real jeweller in the man who knows the worth of a jewel even when he gets it cheap."

"Mashima, you've made the whole thing too subtle—it is like sharpening the psychological edge of a short story. The matter is sufficiently blunt. As happens in this human world, a certain gentleman is crazy on marrying a certain lady. Taking good and bad together, the boy is passable; about the girl it is superfluous to say anything. In the normal course of things such an event should cause merriment and festivity among the tribe of Mashimas."

"Don't you be afraid, my boy. The festivities are about to begin. Take it that you have got Labanya. If, even when she is yours, you continue to want her as much as before, I shall know that you are worthy of a girl like Labanya."

"I thought I was ultra-modern, but you stagger me."

"What sign of the modern do you perceive?"

"Twentieth-century Mashimas seem to be afraid to give in marriage."

"The reason is that the last-century Mashimas gave away dolls in marriage. The modern candidates for marriage are not interested in providing puppets for the amusement of Mashimas."

"You need have no fear. One can never have too much. On the contrary the appetite grows by what it feeds on. To illustrate this truth by marrying Labanya is the sole purpose of Amit Roy's descent to earth. Otherwise why should a motor car—an insentient thing—have brought about such a fantastic, impossible accident on a fantastic spot at a fantastic moment?"

"My boy, your words don't as yet bear witness to a marriageable age. I am afraid the whole thing may turn out in the end to be a mere child wedding."

"Mashima, my mind has a specific gravity of its own by virtue of which the weighty words of my heart sit light on my tongue. But that does not make their weight any the less."

Yogamaya went to see to the arrangements for lunch. Amit wandered from room to room but could not find what he wanted to see. He came upon Jatishankar, and recalled that he was to have read *Antony and Cleopatra* with him that day. A look at Amit's face made it clear to Jati that his immediate duty was to pity this creature and ask leave for the day. He said, "If you don't mind, Amitda, I want leave for the day to hike over Upper Shillong."

Amit was overjoyed and replied:

"Those who know not how to take leave of their lessons merely read without digesting. Why are you so absurdly afraid that I shall mind your asking for a holiday?"

"Tomorrow being Sunday is in any case a holiday. You might think—"

"No, brother! Mine is not the schoolmaster's mind. I don't call a scheduled day a holiday. To enjoy a scheduled holiday is like hunting a tethered animal. The enjoyment palls."

Jati guessed the real cause of Amit Kumar's sudden enthusiasm for the philosophy of holidays, and found it very amusing. He remarked:

"Of late your brain has been much occupied with the philosophy of holidays. The other day too you gave me a lecture on it. If it goes on like this, in a few days I shall have become an adept at leave-taking."

"What was I preaching the other day?"

"You said that the inclination to do what one should not do is a great human virtue. One should never delay to respond to its call. So saying, you closed the book and hurried out. Maybe an inspiration against duty was lurking outside, although I didn't notice it."

Jati was in his teens. The tumult in Amit's blood had not left him unaffected. He had always thought of Labanya as a teacher, but now looking at her through Amit's experience he realized that she was a woman.

Amit laughed. "When work is to be done, one should be ever ready. This exhortation fetches a high price in the market like a sovereign carrying Akbar's signet. But on the other side should be engraved: When no-work raises its banner one should face its challenge with heroism."

"Your heroism is a little too much in evidence these days."

Patting Jati's back Amit remarked,

"When your life's calendar announces the auspicious Ashtami, do not tarry, worship the goddess, sacrifice all urgent work at her altar. For Vijya Dashami will follow in no time, and the goddess will depart."

Jati went away. Puck was about, but she who could justify his presence was nowhere to be seen. Amit went outside.

The climbing rose was laden with blossom. On one side was a profusion of sunflowers, on the other were chrysanthemums in square, wooden pots. At the upper end of the sloping meadow stood a tall eucalyptus. Labanya sat leaning against its trunk with her feet outstretched, wrapped in an ash-coloured shawl. The morning sun shone on her feet. On the kerchief in her lap lay scattered fragments of bread and broken walnuts. She had meant to devote the morning to animal-feeding but had forgotten all about it. Amit came and stood beside her. She raised her head, looked at him and remained silent. A faint smile hovered on her face. Amit sat down facing her.

"Good news. I've got Mashima's consent."

Without replying, Labanya threw a bit of broken walnut at a nearby peach tree, now peachless. Immediately a squirrel slipped down the trunk. This creature was one of the crowd that waited on Labanya's dole.

"If you don't object, let me prune your name a little."

"Do so."

"I shall call you Banyâ."

"Banya?"

"No, no, that might sound like a calumny.[1] A name like that would suit me. I shall call you Banyâ. What say you?"

"By all means—but not in your Mashima's presence."

"Of course not. Such names are like esoteric *mantras,* not to be uttered before others. This one is for my tongue and your ear alone."

"So be it."

"I too must have an unofficial name. What about Brahmaputra? Suddenly the flood comes and causes it to overflow."

"Too heavy for everyday use."

---
1. Banya, wild; Banya, a flood.

Farewell my Friend

"You are right. One would need a coolie to carry it. You had better give me a name. Let it be your creation."

"Very well let me also prune your name and call you Mita."[1]

"Excellent. In Vaishnav poetry its companion name is Bandhu. Banyâ, why not call me by that name before everybody? What harm is there?"

"Fear lest the treasure meant for one ear sound cheap when passed from ear to ear."

"Not untrue. What is intact between two, becomes fragmented between many. Banyâ!"

"Yes, Mita?"

"If I were to compose a poem about your name, do you know how I should rhyme it? *Ananya.*"

"What may that mean?"

"It means that you are what you are and nothing but that."

"There's nothing particularly astounding about that."

"How can you say that? It is astounding—very much so. It is only by rare good luck that one comes across an individual who startles one into exclaiming: She is

---

[1]. Intimate friend, very much like mon ami in French

absolutely herself—and not like half-a-dozen others. That is what I shall say in my poem—

> *Banyâ, your uniqueness*
> *Is blessed in its loveliness.*"

"You are not going to write a poem, are you?"

"Of course. Who is to stop me?"

"What has made you so desperate?"

"I'll tell you. Last night till 2.30 a.m. I was turning from page to page of the *Oxford Book of Verve,* like a man in insomnia turning from this side to that. I couldn't for my life come across a single love poem, though formerly they turned up at every step. It's now clear to me that the whole world is waiting for me to write one."

So saying he caught hold of Labanya's left hand and held it between both of his. "My hands are clasped," he said, "how shall I hold the pen? The best rhyme is the rhyming of hands. These your fingers, how they whisper into mine! No poet could ever write so simply and with such spontaneity."

"You are so fastidious, Mita, that I am afraid of you."

"But just consider my case. Ramchandra wanted to test Sita's virtue by means of fire—the visible, material fire. The result was that he lost Sita. The virtue of a poem too has to be tested in fire, but that fire must be of the mind. How is a man with no fire in his mind going to apply the test? He will have to go by what others say and very often what they say is mere slanderous gossip. My mind today is all fire. By that fire I am reading again all that I have ever read. How little of it survives! Most of it will be burnt to ashes. I must stand up in the noisy market-place of the poets and protest—Don't you shout and bluster. Say the right word and say it softly.

For God's sake hold your tongue and let me love!"

For a long while the two remained seated in silence. Lifting Labanya's hand in his own Amit passed it gently over his own face and said:

"Just consider, Banyâ, on this very morning, at this very moment, what numberless people on this earth are yearning— and how very few of them have got what they desire! I am one of those very few. And you alone in this whole world have seen this fortunate man in one corner of this Shillong hill—under this eucalyptus tree. The most wonderful things on this earth come on tiptoe, evading attention. Yet when any Tom, Dick or Harry, from the Gol-dighi in Calcutta to Noakhali or Chittagong, shrieks slogans, shakes his fist at the empty air and fires off blank cartridges of crooked politics, this atrociously silly news is acclaimed as the most significant news in Bengal. Perhaps it is just as well. Who knows!"

"What is just as well?"

"This, that though life's best prizes cross and recross our most crowded ways, they are not crushed and defiled by the stare of the vulgar. A profound awareness of it pulsates in the deeps of the universe!—Well, Banyâ, I am chattering away, but you are silently brooding. Tell me what you are thinking of."

Labanya continued to sit silent with downcast eyes.

"Your silence," said Amit, "is like dismissing my words without their wages."

Without raising her head Labanya replied:

"When I listen to your words, I am overwhelmed with fear, Mita."

"Fear of what?"

"What exactly you want of me, and how little I can give you—I am at a loss to understand."

"It's precisely because you can give without thinking that your gift is precious."

"When you told me that the Kartama[1] had given her consent, fear seized me, fear of being caught and exposed."

---
1. Term of address for the lady of the house.

"Caught you shall be."

"Mita, your taste, your intellect, are far ahead of mine. If I walk with you on the same road, a day will come when I shall have lagged far behind. Then you will no longer look back and beckon to me. Nor shall I blame you then— no, no, don't interrupt, listen first to what I have to say. I beg of you, do not wish to marry me.

Trying to loosen the tie after marriage will only add to the mess. What I have received from you is enough for me. It will last till the end of my life. But please do not deceive yourself."

"Banyâ, why are you raising the spectre of tomorrow's niggardliness into this days's munificence?"

"Mita, you have given me the strength to speak the truth. Your own heart bears witness to what I am telling you today. You are unwilling to confess the fact lest the slightest doubt mar your enjoyment of the present. You are not the one to set up a household. You are in quest of whatever will quench your fancy's thirst. That is why you flit from literature to literature and that is why you have come to me. Shall I speak the truth? In your heart of hearts you consider marriage, as you are always calling it, vulgar. It's too respectable; it's the luxury of all those scripture-quoting wordlings, the kind who loll on fat cushions and reckon their wives among their goods and chattels."

"Banyâ, you can say astonishingly hard things in astonishingly gentle tones."

"Mita, may I ever be hard in the strength of my love, so that even though I charm you I may never cheat you. Be what you are and love me only as much as your taste permits, and take no obligations on yourself—then I shall be happy."

"Let me have my say now, Banyâ. How wonderfully you have described my character! I shan't argue over that. But in one thing you are mistaken. Even the thing we call man's character changes. As a domestic animal he presents an appearance of chain-bound immobility. But when one day the chain snaps by a sudden stroke of luck and he gallops off into the forest, he is an altogether different sight."

"Which of them are you today?"

"The one which does not match with my usual self. I have met many girls before this—on the paved banks of canalised social intercourse, in the dim light of the shaded lantern of cultivated taste, where one meets without coming to know. Tell me yourself, Banyâ, is my meeting with you of that sort?"

Labanya was silent.

"Two stars," continued Amit, "go round and round each

other, salaaming from a safe, respectable distance. Very decent the law and very innocuous—thus to gravitate in patterned rotation, without the hearts ever meeting. Then without warning the fatal blow falls, their two separate lanterns go out and they crash into each other in one single conflagration! In such a fire has Amit Roy changed. Such is the history of man. It has the appearance of a continuous flow but is in reality a string of incidents. Creation moves under the impact of a succession of such shocks, the quick rhythm of such jolts ushering in one age after another. Banyâ, you have transformed the rhythm of my life and in that rhythm your music and mine are now blended into one."

Labanya's eyelashes were wet. She could not rid her mind of the thought that the frame of Amit's mind was literary, each experience rolling a wave of words to his mouth. That was his life's harvest and the source of his happiness. Hence his need of her. She supplied the warmth which helped to melt the frozen load of unuttered thoughts weighing on his mind. After an interval of long silence, Labanya suddenly asked:

"Don't you think, Mita, that the day the Taj Mahal was completed, Shahjahan must have rejoiced at the death of Mumtaz? Her death was her love's greatest gift. In the Taj Mahal is embodied not Shahjahan's sorrow but his joy."

"Every moment," said Amit, "your words spring a surprise on me. You are undoubtedly a poet."

"I have no desire to be one."

"Why not?"

"My mind refuses to use up the warmth of life in merely lighting a lamp of words. Words are for those who have received command to adorn the hall of life for its festivities. But my life's warmth is for the work of life."

"You repudiate words, Banyâ? Are you not aware how your words have brought me awakening? How can you guess what power there is in your words? Once more I see that I must call in Nibaran Chakravarty. Repeated references to his name have vexed you, but what can I do? The fellow is the keeper of my heart's language. Nibaran has not yet become old and hackneyed to himself. Each time he writes a poem, that is his first poem. Rummaging through his manuscript the other day, I came across a recent composition—a poem on a Waterfall. I wonder how he came to know that I have at last discovered my waterfall in these hills of Shillong. He writes:

> *Waterfall, in the transparent flow*
> *Of thy crystal-clear waters,*
> *The sun and the stars behold themselves.*

Had I written it myself, I couldn't have described you

more vividly. Such a transparency is in your mind that the light of the sky is easily reflected therein. I can see that light shining in everything about you—in your face, in your smile, in your words, when you are seated in repose or when you walk along the road.

Let my shadow this day
Swing and play upon thy waters.
And do thou mingle with that shadow
The music of thy laughter,
And give it voice—the voice
That is thine in eternity.

You are the Waterfall, you not only move with the stream of life, but you also speak as you move. The hard immobile stones over which you leap and bound break into music as you strike against them.

In one image are blended
My shadow and thy laughter,
And lo! my heart has caught
The poet's frenzy.
Step by step, moment by moment,
The gleam of thy light endows my heart with speech,
O waterfall.
I see myself today as voice incarnate—

*At thy swift touch my mind awakes,
I know myself."*

Smiling wanly Labanya remarked, "For all my light and my music, your shadow remains a shadow, beyond my power to hold."

"Perhaps one day you will see that if anything of mine has survived, it is the voice incarnate."

"Where?" laughed Labanya. "In the manuscript of Nibaran Chakravarty?"

"Why not? The stream that flows in the deepest layer of my mind somehow finds an outlet through Nibaran's fountain."

"Then perhaps one day I shall find your mind only in that fountain of Nibaran Chakravarty's, and nowhere else."

At this moment a servant came and announced that the food was ready.

Amit pondered as he walked. "Labanya wants to analyse everything in the light of the intellect. She is unable to deceive herself even in the field where it is most natural to deceive oneself. I cannot refute what she said. Men must find an outlet for the intimate realizations of their inner consciousness. Some find it in life and some in creative composition—now touching life, now falling back, as the river continually touches and falls back from its banks. Must I be always falling back from life, swept along in the current of literary creation? Is that the difference between man and woman? Man to attain the fulfilment of his powers in creative activity—the creative urge deceiving itself at every step to further its own progress? And woman to spend her powers in conserving, in obstructing new creations, to protect the old? Creation is merciless to preservation, which is but an obstacle in its way. Why must it be thus—that somewhere the two must inevitably clash? The place of their most intimate union is the core of a great hostility. Hence it seems to me that our highest fulfilment lies not in union but in freedom."

Painful as these thoughts were to Amit, his mind could not disown them.

Labanya Argues

Yogamaya said, "Labanya dear, are you sure you have understood?"

"Indeed I have, mother."

"That Amit is very wayward, I admit; that is why I am so fond of him. Don't you see how distraught he looks—as though everything is about to slip away from him!"

"If he had to retain everything," replied Labanya, smiling, "if things did not slip away from his hand, it would indeed prove a misfortune for him. The law of his being is that either he will not get what he is about to get, or will lose it as soon as he gets it. That he should hold what he gets does not tally with his nature."

"To tell you the truth, my child, I do greatly like his childish irresponsible ways."

"That happens to be the mother's way. The brunt of childishness is borne wholly by the mother, while the fun of it is enjoyed by the child. But why ask me to bear the burden? Why thrust it on one unable to stand it?"

"But haven't you noticed, Labanya, how subdued his mind has become of late—his mind which was so wild and wayward before? I find the sight very touching. Say what you will, he does love you."

"'That he does."

"Then why worry?"

"Because I have no wish to play the tyrant with his nature."

"All I know, Labanya, is that love partly welcomes, partly practises, tyranny."

"Such tyranny has its limits. Where it represses nature, it overreaches itself. The more I read of love in literature the more I feel convinced that the tragedy of love is brought about where the two are not content to accept the fact of each other's individuality, where each strives to impose his will on the other, where I seek to mould the other in the image of my own desire."

"For the matter of that, dear, it's hardly possible for two

to make one family without to some extent moulding each other. Where there is love, such moulding is easy enough. Where love is absent, the use of the hammer brings about what you call tragedy."

"We are not discussing a man who is made for family life. Such a man is like clay, he is automatically moulded into shape by the daily pressure of circumstances. But a man who has no clay in his nature cannot possibly give up his individuality. If the woman fails to realize this, the more she claims the more she will lose; if the man fails to realize this, the more he grabs the more he will miss the real mate of his heart. It's my belief that most often what we call getting is no other than the handcuffs getting the hand."

"What exactly do you want, Labanya?"

"I don't want to marry and cause unhappiness. Matrimony is not for all. You know, Kartama, persons of fastidious temperament pull the individual to pieces, picking up a bit here, discarding a bit there. But once caught in the net of marriage, man and woman are dragged too close to each other—no gap is left between them. Then one is obliged to work with the other as he or she is, and at very close range. There is no means of hiding even a portion of one's self."

"You do not know yourself, Labanya. No one need reject anything of you."

"But he does not want *me.* He does not seem even to have noticed—me the everyday person, me the girl at home. No sooner did I touch his mind than it bubbled forth in an endless stream of words. With words he seeks to remould me. If his mind wearies, if the words fail him, this very commonplace girl who was not his own creation will be exposed in that void. Marriage means acceptance, which leaves little room for moulding on the potter's wheel."

"Do you think that Amit will not be able to take a girl like you as you are?"

"He may accept me if his nature changes. But why should it change? I don't want that."

"What then do you want?"

"I want to remain a dream as long as I may, blended with his words, with the play of his fancy. Indeed, why should I call it a dream, when it is for me a unique rebirth, a unique revelation of self in a unique world? What if it is only a colourful butterfly come out of its cocoon for a brief sojourn—What harm is there in it? Is a butterfly less real than other things in this world? What if it rises with the sun and dies with the sunset? What of it? All that matters is that the brief interval should not be in vain."

"Very well, let's take it that to Amit you are only a passing vision. What of yourself? Do you also want never to marry? Is Amit an illusion to you also?"

Labanya sat silent. No word came from her. Yogamaya continued.

"When you argue, I can see that you have read a great deal. I can neither think like you nor talk like you. Perhaps I can't even dare like you. But I have been watching you, dear, even through the very gaps in your dialectic. The other day—it was near midnight—seeing the light burning in your room, I went in and found you crying, your head sunk on the table, your face hidden in your hands. You were no philosopher-maiden then. For a moment I thought, let me console her. But then I said to myself, every woman must weep out her grief when the day of weeping comes; it's no use suppressing it. I know well that you want to love with the heart, not to create with the mind. Unless you can pour out your heart and soul in devotion, how can you survive? That is why, I say, you need must have him near you. Don't pledge yourself hastily to forswear marriage. I fear your obstinacy—once you've made up your mind, it's impossible to change you."

Labanya remained mute. With head bent she kept on needlessly pressing and folding the loose end of her sari in her lap. Yogamaya went on.

"When I watch you, it often seems to me that much reading and thinking has made the minds of young people subtle. You have built up within yourselves a mental pattern that has no correspondence to this world of ours. You can't do without these mental rays that pierce the solid curtain of the body, as though flesh and blood were not there. In our days such rays were unknown, but our own crude ideas sufficed for the joys and sorrows of life; and even then problems were plentiful. But nowadays you have raised and multiplied them so much that nothing remains simple any longer."

Labanya smiled. Only the other day Amit was explaining to Yogamaya all about the invisible rays, and that was how she had got this particular argument into her head. This too was subtlety. Yogamaya's mother couldn't have understood the thing in that way. She said:

"Kartama, the more clearly we discern the working of the time-process, the better able are we to resist its shocks. The agony of darkness is so intolerable because it is obscure."

"It seems to me now," said Yogamaya, "that it would have been better if you two had never met."

"No, no, don't say that. I can't even bear to think of anything happening other than what has happened. At one time I was convinced that I was absolutely dried up—destined to spend my life in reading books and passing exams. I know now that I too can love. The great thing is that the impossible has become possible. I feel I was only a shadow before. Now I am real. What more can I want? But please, Kartama, don't ask me to marry."

So saying she slipped down from the chair and, hiding her face in Yogamaya's lap, began to weep.

Change of Abode

At first every one was sure that Amit would be back in Calcutta within a fortnight. Naren Mitter had even betted heavily that Amit couldn't stand a week of Shillong. But a month passed, two months passed, and there was no word of his return. The lease of the Shillong house expired; a Zamindar from Rangpur came and took possession of it. After a good deal of search a cottage near Yogamaya's house was secured. At one time it had been inhabited by a cowherd or a gardener; later on by a clerk who imparted to it a touch of impecunious respectability. The clerk being dead, his widow now let out the cottage. So niggardly was its supply of doors and windows that the three elements, heat, light and air could hardly get in, though on a rainy day the fourth element penetrated in overwhelming profusion through innumerable obscure inlets.

Seeing, the state of the room one day, Yogamaya was shocked.

"What ordeal have you imposed on yourself, my boy?" she exclaimed.

"Uma's penance," replied Amit, "consisted in depriving herself of food; in the end she gave up eating even leaves. Mine consists in depriving myself of the use of all furniture, renouncing one by one, bedstead, couch, table, chair, till I am reduced to these blank walls. Her penance was in the Himalayas, mine amid the hills of Shillong. There a bride wanted a groom, here a groom wants a bride. There Narad was the match-maker, here Mashima herself is present. Now if it should happen that no Kalidasa[1] turns up, I shall necessarily have to carry on his work as best as I can."

Amit laughed as he talked, but his words grieved Yogamaya. She wanted to invite him to her house, but restrained herself. "In this drama of destiny our interference may only add impossible complications," she thought. Instead she sent down a few things from her own establishment,

---

1. Reference to the Sanskrit poet's famous narrative poem, Kumarasambhava, describing the marriage of Siva with Parvati (Uma).

and her pity for this castaway was simultaneously redoubled. She kept on remonstrating: "Labanya dear, do not turn your heart to stone."

One day after a very heavy shower Yogamaya came down to inquire how Amit was faring. She found him seated on a blanket underneath a rickety table, poring over an English book. Seeing his room inundated by an unseemly intrusion of water, Amit had fortified his table as a sort of cave and was sprawling beneath it. First he had a good laugh all to himself after which began the enjoyment of poetry. His mind flew towards Yogamaya's house, but the body could not follow; the reason being that in Calcutta, where it was not needed, he had bought a very expensive rain-coat which he had forgotten to bring where it was constantly needed. True, he had brought an umbrella with him, but very likely he had left it behind at the very place to which his imagination now turned, or, may be, it was still lying at the foot of the old deodar. Entering the room Yogamaya exclaimed :

"Whatever is the matter, Amit?"

Emerging hastily from under the table, Amit replied, "My room today is deliriously incoherent, its condition little better than mine."

"Deliriously incoherent?"

"In other words, the roof of this dwelling may be likened

to India. There is little coherence between its parts; if there's an outrage from above, there's a regular riot of tears all over the place; and if there's a gust of wind from outside, there rises within a chorus of sighs. By way of protest, I have improvised a platform over my head—an example of unperturbed Home-rule in the midst of misgovernment. It illustrates a fundamental principle of politics."

"What fundamental principle?"

"The self-help improvised by a poor tenant is more effective than the rule of an absentee landlord, however potent."

Today Yogamaya was very wroth with Labanya. The deeper grew her affection for Amit, the higher she raised him on the pedestal of her mind. "Such learning, such intellect, such qualifications, and yet so unaffected! What amazing gift of expression! As for looks, he seems to me far better-looking than Labanya. She is lucky indeed that by some conspiracy of the stars Amit's eyes are so charmed by her. Fancy her torturing such a jewel of a boy. She declared without rhyme or reason that she won't marry, as if she were an empress, for whom warriors must break the bow. Insufferable vanity. The wretched girl is marked out for tragedy."

For a moment she thought of taking Amit with her in the

car to her own house. On second thought, however, she merely said:

"Just wait a while, my boy. I'll be back in no time."

On returning home she found Labanya in her room, reclining on a sofa, her feet tucked under a shawl, reading Gorki's *Mother*. Seeing her so snugly comfortable, Yogamaya grew even more angry in her mind.

"Come, let's go out for a while."

"I don't feel like going out today, Kartama."

How could Yogamaya know that Labanya had sought refuge in the book only to escape from her own self! The whole afternoon, after lunch, she had waited restlessly for Amit. Every now and again her heart said, here he comes! Outside the pines swayed and staggered from time to time under the impact of the violent wind, and the infant torrents released by the tempestuous rain rushed impetuously, gasping for breath, as though they must race against the brief term of their life. Labanya felt an irrepressible urge to break all barriers, dispel all misgivings, seize both Amit's hands and confess, I am yours in life and death. Such a declaration would come easy today. The very sky howls a desperate, incomprehensible challenge, and in it the woods and the forests have found their speech. The mountain peaks behind their screen of falling rain are straining their ears to listen to it. Like them let a listener come to hear Labanya's speech, in the same profound stillness, with the same pervasive attention. But hour after hour goes by and no one comes. The moment of the heart's great Aye is past, and once it is gone the listener comes in vain, the word cannot be spoken, the misgivings will reappear, the frenzied rhythm of the cosmic dance that cast out fear from the heart has dissolved into thin air. Year after year passes in silence and once only comes the hour when speech unlooked-for knocks at the human door. If then the key that should open it is missing, never again will the divine gift of the dauntless word be vouchsafed. On such a day one longs to take the whole world into confidence—Listen ye all, I love! I love! The words come like an unknown bird from beyond the seas, journeying from afar, flying for days and nights. For them the divinity within me has kept its vigil. At their touch my whole life, my whole universe, have found their meaning. Labanya hid her face in her pillow and murmured—to whom? "This is the truth, the truth, the only truth."

Time passed. The guest did not come. The heavy load of waiting crushed her heart in pain. Going out on the veranda Labanya let the gusts of rain wet her a little. Then in utter dejection she wrapped up her mind in deep despair. It seemed to her that the light of her life gave one flicker and was gone, blotting out her universe. The courage of inward conviction by which she could have accepted Amit as he was now deserted her. The supreme faith of love which had been hers faded away. After a long stupor she picked up a book from the table. It took time to adjust the mind, but once it was drawn into the interest of the story she unconsciously lost herself in it—when suddenly Yogamaya came and asked her to go out. She had not the heart to do so.

Pulling up a chair Yogamaya seated herself in front of Labanya and fixing flashing eyes on her face asked:

"Tell me the truth, Labanya. Do you love Amit?"

"Why do you ask such a question, Kartama?" asked Labanya, hurriedly sitting up.

"If you don't love him, why don't you tell him so plainly? You are callous. If you don't want him, then don't hold him."

Labanya's heart choked within her; she could not speak.

"What I saw of him just now is enough to break one's heart. For whose sake is he rotting here like a beggar? How can you be totally blind to it? A girl wooed by such a boy ought to thank her stars."

Struggling to control her choking breath, Labanya replied, "You ask me about love, Kartama? I can't imagine any one could love more than I do. I would give up my life for love. All that I was is wiped out. This is a new beginning for me, a beginning with no end. Such a marvel has sprung to life in me! How can I explain it to others? Could anyone else feel as I do?"

Yogamaya was stunned. She had always seen Labanya completely self-possessed. Where had all the turbulent passion been hidden?

Softly, gently, Yogamaya spoke. "Labanya dear, do not suppress yourself. Amit is looking for you in darkness, let him see you as you are in all your completeness, don't be afraid. If only he could see the light that is in you he would need nothing. Come, dear, come with me right now." The two set out for Amit's cottage.

10

Second Sadhana

Spreading a number of newspaper sheets over the wet seat Amit settled down in his chair. A sheaf of foolscap sheets in front of him, he had just commenced to write his much talked-of autobiography. If questioned about it he would have replied that his life had only now revealed itself to him in all its multi-coloured hues, like the hills of Shillong on a morning after the rain. Now that he had realized the worth of his existence, how could he help revealing it? According to Amit, the reason why a man's biography is generally written after his death is that it is only when he is dead to the world, that he begins to live again in the minds of men. Thereby Amit implied that while one aspect of him had died in Shillong his past fading away like a mirage, in another aspect he was reborn intensely alive, an image of resplendent light against the background of darkness. It was desirable to announce such a revelation, for very few on this earth are fortunate enough to experience it. Most lives drag on from birth to death in the shadow of twilight, like bats in a cave.

It was drizzling mildly, the tempest had subsided, the clouds had dispersed.

"How unfair of you, Mashima!" cried Amit, jumping up from his chair.

"Why, what have I done?"

"I am caught absolutely unprepared. What will Srimati Labanya think?"

"It's necessary to make Srimati Labanya think a little. It's good to know what ought to be known. Why should Sriyukta Amit be nervous?"

"Let the Srimati see the Sriyukta in his glory only. The beggars' penury may be exposed only to the Mashima."

"Why such discrimination, son?"

"In my own interest. One may claim riches only by offering riches. The utmost that indigence can claim is sympathy. Civilization owes its glory to Labanya Devis and its humanity to Mashimas!"

"One can have both Devi and Mashima in one, Amit. It may not be necessary to hide one's indigence."

"To which an answer can be given only in the words of a poet. What I say in prose needs a commentary in verse. Matthew Arnold has called poetry criticism of life. By way of emendation I should like to call it life's commentary in verse. For the benefit of my honoured guest, I should state beforehand that what I am going to recite is by no prince among poets.

> *Do not seek with empty hands*
> *What should be sought with the whole heart,*
> *Nor with wet eyes stand at its door.*

Just consider. Love itself is wealth, its longings are not the hankerings of a pauper. When God loves a devotee He comes to his door in the garb of a beggar.

> *In the abundance of your giving*
> *Shall the garlands be exchanged.*
> *Will you spread your goddess' seat*
> *On the dust of the wayside?*

That is why I asked the lady just now to be considerate before entering the room. What shall I spread for her when I have nothing to spread? These wet newspaper sheets? I fear the stain of editorial ink. The poet says: I do not invite the object of my heart to share my thirst; I invite when the cup of life is overflowing.

In Vaisakh[1] when the woods shrivel
In the blasting devouring wind,
Will you fill with withered flowers
Your basket of love's offering?
With the full splendour of your spirit
Welcome the guest your heart has invited,
Let the lamps with their thousand tongues of light
Chase away all darkness.

Man's first tapasya comes in infancy when the naked sannyasi lies helpless in his Mashima's lap. That is his first sadhana, his first training in tenderness. This cottage represents the same stern preparation. I have already made up my mind to name this cottage Mashian Bungalow."

"The second tapasya of life, my son, is of glory—the sadhana of love, with the maiden by one's side. This sadhana of yours is taking place in this cottage, and no number of wet newspaper sheets can damp it. Must you delude yourself that the boon is not yet granted? Surely you know in your heart of hearts that you have got it!"

So saying she made Labanya stand by Amit's side and

---

1. April-May when the hot winds blow.

taking her right hand placed it over his. She unclasped the golden necklace from Labanya's neck and fastened it over their hands, exclaiming: "May your union abide!"

Both Amit and Labanya bent down and took the dust of Yogamaya's feet. She said, "Please wait for me here while I go and fetch flowers from the garden." She went by car to get the flowers.

For a long time the two remained silent, seated side by side on the cot. Then raising her face to Amit's Labanya asked,

"Why didn't you come today?"

"The reason," replied Amit, "is so slight that one must be bold indeed to mention it on a day like this. It is nowhere mentioned in history that for want of a raincoat the lover had to defer his visit to his beloved. On the contrary it is stated that he swam across the unfathomable ocean. That, however, refers to the history of the heart in whose deep waters I too am swimming. Shall I ever traverse that shoreless ocean?

> *For we are bound where mariner has not yet dared to go,*
> *And we will risk the ship, ourselves and all.*

Were you waiting for me today, Banyâ?"

"Indeed, I was, Mita. The whole day I listened to your

footsteps in the patter of the rain. It seemed to me that you were coming from the very ends of the earth. At long last you have entered my life."

"Banyâ, right in the centre of my life there has gaped till now the huge black chasm of my not knowing you. That was the ugliest spot of all. Today it is filled to the brim; on it the light shimmers and in it all the heavens are reflected. Today it is the loveliest spot of all. This my ceaseless prattle is but an echo of the waves on that overfilled lake of life. Who can silence it?"

"Mita, how did you pass your time today?"

"In the centre of my consciousness, poised in absolute stillness, were you. I was going to say something to you, but where are the words gone? The rain pours from above, while I sit and repeat, give me words, the word!

> *O what is this?*
> *Mysterious and uncapturable bliss*
> *That I have known, yet seems to be*
> *Simple as breath and easy as a smile,*
> *And older than the earth.*

That's my occupation—making others' words my own. Had I the gift of a composer, I would have set to music Vidyapati's song of the rains and made it entirely my own.

*Says Vidyapati, how shall I beguile
My nights and days without the Lord?*

How can the days pass without one who is the life of my life? Where am I to get the right music for these words? I raise my eyes and pray, now for words, now for music. With words and music the god does descend, but on the way he mistakes the individual and without rhyme or reason hands over both music and words to an altogether different person—perhaps to that Rabindranath Tagore of yours."

Labanya laughed. "Even those who love Rabindranath do not recall him as often as you do."

"Banyâ, I am talking too much today, am I not? A monsoon of garrulity has burst within me. If you were to keep note of the weather reports you would be staggered at the vagaries of my eccentricity. If we had been in Calcutta I would have taken you in a car and raced straight to Moradabad, bursting tyres galore on the way. If you had asked, why Moradabad? I couldn't have told you why. When the flood comes it roars and races and sweeps time along, like foam, with its laughter."

At this moment Yogamaya entered with a basket full of sunflowers and said: "Labanya dear, touch his feet today with these flowers." A feminine attempt to embody in a ceremony what was in the heart. This hankering for form is in the very blood and bones of women.

Amit seized an opportune moment to whisper into Labanya's ear.

"Banyâ, I must get a ring for you."

"Why, Mita? Is it necessary?"

"By placing this hand of yours in mine you have given me more than I can dream of. Poets talk only of the face of the beloved; but what a wealth of suggestion is in the hand! All the endearments of love, its devotion, its tenderness, its unutterable longing, are in the hand. This ring will wrap itself round your finger like a tiny word of my heart. Just this. Mine! Let this my little word ever cling to your hand—in the speech of gold, in the speech of precious stone."

"Very well, as you wish."

"I'll send for it from Calcutta. Tell me, which stone do you fancy?"

"No stone. A pearl will do."

"Excellent. I too love pearls."

II

Love's Philosophy

❦

It was settled that the wedding would take place in the month of Agrahayana and that Yogamaya was to go to Calcutta to make the necessary arrangements.

Said Labanya to Amit, "You were due back in Calcutta long ago. Now that your mind is freed of doubt and suspense, you may go without any misgiving. We shan't meet before the wedding."

"Why this severe discipline?"

"The other day you talked of the simplicity of happiness. Well, to preserve this simplicity."

"These are words of profound wisdom. The other day

I suspected you of being a poet; today I suspect you of being a philosopher. You have said it superbly. One has to be severe to preserve the natural ease of the simple. If you want ease and simplicity of rhythm you have to strain hard to keep the pauses in the right place. In our excess of greed we fight shy of restraint in the poetry of life. The rhythm is marred and life becomes a unmusical bondage. All right, I'll leave tomorrow, tear myself away from these rich overflowing days. It'll be like that verse in *Meghnadvadh Kavya*—*so* startlingly and untimely arrested:

—*When to the land of death he went Untimely.*

However, though I may be obliged to leave Shillong, the month of Agrahayana cannot abscond from the calendar. Can you guess what I shall do in Calcutta?"

"What will you do?"

"While Mashima is busy with arrangements for the wedding day, I shall occupy myself with arrangements for the days after. People forget that the married life is an art; each day it is to be fashioned anew. Do you remember, Banyâ, the description of Indumati by Maharaja Aja in *Raghuvamsa?*"

"Dearest disciple in every loving art," Labanya quoted.

"This loving art is of the wedded life. The vulgar

identify wedding with union, with the result that the real union of the two is neglected after the wedding."

"Do expound to me your conception of the art of union. If you want me to be your disciple, let the first lesson begin today."

"Very well, then listen. By voluntarily accepting restraint the poet creates rhythm. The union of the two is similarly to be made beautiful by a voluntary acceptance of restraint. To take for granted is to cheapen what is priceless and thereby to deceive oneself. The joy of paying a heavy price is great indeed."

"Let's hear how you reckon the price."

"Wait a bit. Let me first tell you of the picture in my mind. The Ganges-bank near Diamond Harbour, a small steam launch to carry one to Calcutta in a couple of hours."

"How does Calcutta come in?"

"Calcutta plays no significant part in my life at present—that you know. True, I go to the Bar Library—not for professional work, but to play chess. The attorneys have understood that not being in need of work, my heart is not in it. They pass on a brief to me only when the case is to be amicably settled. But after marriage, I am going to show them what it is to work—

not for the sake of livelihood but for the sake of life. At the core of a mango is the stone, which is neither sweet, nor soft, nor edible, but whose hardness is nevertheless the very prop of the mango, the basis of its form. The stony hardness of Calcutta is necessary—do you now understand for what? To keep the hard core in the midst of sweetness."

"I understand. That makes it equally necessary for me too. Shall I also have to go to Calcutta—from 10 a.m. to 5 p.m.?"

"Why not? Not to gad about, but to work."

"What sort of work? Honorary?"

"Certainly not. Honorary work is neither work nor pleasure, but a positive farce. If you like you can accept a professorship, in a women's college."

"Very well, I shall like it then. What else?"

"I can see it vividly. The Ganges bank. From its lowest slope rises an ancient, hoary banyan tree, with its many descending proproots. When Dhanapati was sailing down the Ganges on his way to Ceylon, may be he moored his boat to this very banyan and cooked his food under its shade. To its right is a paved ghat overlaid with moss, dilapidated, with cracks all over. At the ghat is our slender boat, green-and-white. On its blue banner the name is painted in white. You had better give it a name."

"Shall I? Mitali."

"Just the right name—Mitali. I had thought of Sagari and was a little proud of it too. But I yield the palm to you. A tiny rivulet flows through the garden—a pulse of the Ganges. On that side of it is your abode, on this mine."

"Will you have to swim across every day and must I keep the light burning by my window?"

"We'll swim in mind, while crossing the pole-bridge. Your abode shall be named Manasi, and mine—you will have to give it a name."

"Dipak."

"The very name. I shall set a lamp, befitting the name, on the crest of the house. On the evening of our union a red light shall glow therein; on the night of separation a blue one. Each day on returning from Calcutta I shall expect your letter—such a letter as may turn up or may not. If I do not get it by eight in the evening, I shall curse my luck and try to read Bertrand Russell's Logic. Our rule being that uninvited I can never visit your abode."

"And I yours?"

"It would be better to keep to the same rule. However, an occasional breach of the rule will not be unwelcome."

"If the breach itself does not become the rule, what a mess your house will be in! Just think of it. I had better come in a burqa."

"As you please. But I shall need a letter of invitation. That letter need contain nothing more than a line or two from a poem."

"And will there be no invitation for me? Shall I be outcasted?"

"You shall be invited once a month, on the full-moon night, when the fragmented beauty of the fourteen days shall attain its full and rounded glory."

"Let your dear disciple have a sample of your letter now."

"Very well."

Taking a note-book from his pocket, Amit tore out a leaf and wrote on it:

Blow gently over my garden
Wind of the southern sea
In the hour my love cometh
And calleth me.

Labanya did not return the note.

"Let me now have," said Amit, "a sample of your letter and see how far your education has progressed."

Labanya was about to write on a scrap of paper, when Amit protested,

"No, you must write in this note-book of mine." Labanya wrote in Sanskrit, quoting from Jayadeva:

> *Mita, thou art my life, my ornament thou,*
> *The very pearl of my life's ocean thou!*

Replacing the book in his pocket, Amit remarked,

"Surprising that I should have quoted a woman's words and you a man's. Nothing unseemly about it. The flame looks the same whether the burning log is from the *simul* tree or from the *bakul*."

"Now that invitations have been exchanged," said Labanya, "what else?"

"The evening star appears, the Ganges swells with the tide, the wind sings in the row of casuarinas, the waters lap on the knotted roots of the hoary banyan. At the back of your house is the lotus-tank, at whose secluded, solitary ghat you have just bathed and dressed your hair. Your sari changes its colour from day to day. As I come, I wonder, what colour will it be this evening? The tryst also varies, today it is on the platform beneath the champak tree, tomorrow on the roof-terrace or the terrace on the Ganges bank. I have bathed in the Ganges and have donned a white muslin dhoti and chaddar and wooden sandals, inlaid with ivory. Arriving I find you seated on a carpet, in front of you a heavy garland on a silver platter, sandalwood paste in a tiny bowl, and incense burning in the corner. At least for a couple of months during the Puja holidays we must go abroad—but to different places. If you go to the hills, I go seawards. These, herewith submitted to you, are the rules and regulations of our domestic dyarchy. What say you of them?"

"I agree to abide by them."

"Between abiding by and accepting there is a difference, Banyâ."

"I will not object to what is necessary to you, even when it is superfluous to me."

"Superfluous to you?"

"Indeed. However near you may be, you are still far away. It is unnecessary for me to have recourse to rules and regulations to maintain that distance. Well I know that there is nothing in me which can stand your close scrutiny without my blushing for shame—which makes the division of domestic life in two different abodes on two opposing banks quite innocuous, as far as I am concerned."

Jumping up from his chair Amit exclaimed:

"I will not be worsted by you, Banyâ. Hang the garden. We won't move a step outside Calcutta. I'll rent an apartment on the top floor of Niranjan's office, at Rs. 75 a month, where you shall live and I too. In the realm of the mind there is no near and no far. On the left side of a five-foot broad bedstead shall be your quarters, the Manasi; on the right side mine, the Dipak. To the east of the room will be an almirah with a mirror, which will reflect your face as well as mine. To the west a bookcase, whose back will shut out the sun and whose front will provide a single circulating library for the two readers. North of the room will be a sofa on one end of which I shall sit, leaving a little room on my left. A few paces away, just behind the clothes rack, you will stand. With a trembling hand I shall hold aloft the invitation letter, whereon shall be written:

> *Blow gently over the terrace*
> *Wind of the South sweet*
> *In the hour my love cometh*
> *And our four eyes meet.*

Does it sound bad, Banyâ?"

"Not at all, Mita. But where did you get it from?"

"From the manuscript of my friend Nilmadhav. His prospective bride was still undetermined. However, inspired by the prospect, he refashioned the English poem in Calcatian mould, wherein I too co-operated. Having secured his M.A. in Economics, he then secured as dowry Rs.15,000 in cash and ornaments weighing 80 tolas, and brought the new bride home and had his fill of the wind of the south sweet and of the four eyes meeting. But for the poem he no longer had any use. Now he wouldn't mind vesting in his partner the full proprietary rights over the poem."

"The southern breeze will blow over your terrace too, but will your new bride always remain a new bride?"

Thumping the table hard Amit shouted aloud.

"She shall! she shall! she shall remain!!!"

"What shall remain?" asked Yogamaya, hurrying from the adjoining room. "Not my table, obviously."

"Whatever deserves to endure shall survive. An ever new bride is a rarity, and if, by the grace of the gods, such a one is found in a million, she shall remain eternally a bride."

"Let's have an example."

"A day will come when I shall show you."

"Apparently it will take time. In the meantime — come and have your food."

12

The Last Evening

❦

The meal over, Amit announced:

"Mashima, I am leaving for Calcutta tomorrow. My kith and kin suspect that I have turned Khasi."[1]

"Do the kith and kin know that you change so easily?"

"Only too well. Why else are they kith and kin? But that doesn't prove that I am such a quick-change artist or capable of turning Khasi. What has happened to me today is not a mere conversion; it's an epochal change, marking

---

1. A hill tribe of that part.

the end of an age. Prajapati has awakened within me to make a new creation. Mashima, please let me take Labanya out today. Let my last salutation to the Shillong hills be joined with hers."

Mashima gave permission. No sooner had they started than hand was gathered in hand and body drew close to body. Beneath the edge of the solitary path stretched a deep forest. Within the forest was a bare spot where the sky had escaped a little from its mountainous confinement, filling both its hands with the departing glory of the setting sun. There the two of them stood facing the west. Amit drew Labanya's head to his breast and lifted up her face. Her eyes were half closed, tears trickling from the corners. The gold of the sky was blending with molten ruby and emerald: between the gaps in the thin clouds were visible glimpses of blue so limpid, so intense, that one could feel flowing through it the silent music of that celestial sphere where there is no flesh, only pure bliss. Slowly it grew dark; in the deepening gloom of the night the little patch of open sky seemed like a flower whose many-coloured petals were closed.

"Let's go back," whispered Labanya from her close proximity to Amit's breast. Somehow she felt that the scene should fittingly close there. Amit understood and said nothing. He clasped Labanya's face in a warmer embrace and then slowly retraced his steps.

"I shall have to leave early tomorrow morning," he said. "I shan't see you again before I go."

"Why not?"

"The Shillong chapter of our life ended today at the right spot. Here endeth the first canto—our Prelude to Paradise."

Labanya said nothing. She walked on, Amit's hand in hers, joy in her heart, yet mingled with a heaviness of tears. She felt that never again for her would the unimaginable be so intimately near. In one supreme moment, the auspicious vision had come; but for her there would follow no bridal chamber, only one last salutation of mingled union and farewell. A great desire seized her to offer that salutation to Amit then and there, saying "Thou has made me blessed." But somehow the words remained unspoken.

As they neared the house Amit said:

"Banyâ, speak your last word today in verse, so that it will be easy for me to remember. Some little thing, whatever comes to your mind."

Labanya thought for a moment, then recited in Bengali:

> *"I brought you no happiness. Only the gift of freedom*
> *I leave behind at the luminous end of the night.*
> *Naught else remains—no importunity,*

No piling of abjectness from moment to moment,
No vanity, no piteous crying, nor proud laughter.
Nor looking back. Only the offering of freedom
Have I filled today from my own great annihilation."

"Very unfair of you, Banyâ. This is not what you should say on a day like this—never! What made you think of it? Please take back your poem—at once!"

"What are you afraid of, Mita? This fire-chastened love makes no claim to happiness. Free itself, it confers freedom. It brings in its train neither weariness nor ennui. What gift can be better?"

"But where did you get this poem from? I want to know."

"From Rabindranath Tagore."

"Never saw it in any of his books." "It's not yet published in a book."

"Then how did you get hold of it?"

"'There was a boy who was deeply devoted to my father, as a disciple to a master. From him he had received food for his intellect. But there was a hunger in his heart which drove him whenever he had time to Rabindranath, to gather from his manuscript a handful of alms."

"And he brought and offered it at your feet."

"That much boldness he lacked. He would just leave it somewhere where it might catch my eye or fall into my hand."

"Were you kind to him?"

"I didn't have the chance. In my heart I pray that God may be kind to him."

"I can well understand that the poem you have recited today was the very voice of that unfortunate heart."

"Indeed, so it was."

"Then what made you think of it today?"

"How can I say? There was another piece too, which also keeps on recurring to my mind today—I don't understand why.

> *Lovely one, you have brought tears to fill the eyes,*
> *And have kindled in my heart the sacrificial fire unbearable,*
> *In that fire sorrow is tempered and it glows,*
> *The spell of the infatuated mind is broken,*
> *And the hundred-petalled lotus of separation*
> *Expands in its warmth into full bloom."*

"Banyâ, why has this boy come between us today? This is not jealousy—I hold jealousy in contempt. Nevertheless a fear fills my mind. Tell me, what made you recall, today of all days, the poems he gave you?"

"One day after he had left us for good I discovered these poems in the desk where he used to sit and write. Besides these, there were several other poems of Rabindranath— almost a bookful. Perhaps these farewell poems have recurred to my mind because I am bidding you farewell."

"Can that farewell be compared with this?"

"How can I say? But why these arguments? I like these poems and therefore read them to you. Perhaps there is no other reason."

"Banyâ, until men have completely forgotten Rabindranath's poems his genuine work will never come into its own. That is why I never use his poems. Popular appreciation is like the mist whose wet hand sullies the light of the sky."

"You see, Mita, the thing that a woman prizes she keeps to herself, locked in her bosom, and does not discuss it with the crowd. She pays all she can, she does not care to bargain in the market."

"Then there is hope for me too, Banyâ. I shall hide away the trivial stamp of my market value and stride about bearing the big seal of your evaluation."

"We are nearly home now, Mita. Let me hear from your lips your poem of the journey's end."

"Don't take it ill, Banyâ, if I do not choose a verse from Tagore."

"Why should I take it ill?"

"I have discovered a poet whose style—"

"I have been hearing of him from you ever since we met. I have written to Calcutta for his books."

"Good Heavens! His books! The fellow has many shortcomings, but publishing books is not one of them. You will gradually come to know him through me, otherwise—"

"Don't be afraid, Mita. I am sure I shall grow to appreciate him as you appreciate him. I shall be the gainer."

"How?"

"What I gain through my own taste is mine and what I gain through yours also becomes mine. My receiving capacity will be of two minds. I shall be able to retain both the poets on the shelf in your little room in Calcutta. Now out with your poem."

"I haven't the heart to recite it now. This interlude of argument and counter-argument has spoiled the atmosphere."

"Not in the least. The atmosphere is all right."

Brushing his hair up with his fingers, Amit began in a very feeling tone:

> *"Lovely One, thou art the morning star*
> *On the far-away mountain crest!*
> *When the night has run its course*
> *Be thou visible still to the vagrant gone astray.*

Do you understand, Banyâ, it's the moon calling to the evening star to keep it company through the night. It's no longer in love with the night.

> *Where the earth meets the sky*
> *I come, the half-awakened moon,*
> *Like a dimly-luminous bruise*
> *On the breast of darkness.*

This semi-wakefulness, this partial luminousness which is but a rent in the darkness, is its sorrow. It is trapped in the net of this triviality and in the struggle to break through is raving in sleep. What an idea! Grand!

> *On the great void sleep-entranced*
> *My seat is spread,*
> *I finger the string as I dream*
> *Ruffling so lightly the trance.*

But the burden of such a slight existence is heavy indeed. The dying river collects only rubbish in its sluggish and weary flow. What is insufficient gathers only affliction of itself. Hence it says:

With slow steps I traverse the path
To the end of my journey.
My music fails me again and again
And weariness benumbs me.

But is this weariness the last word? The hope of tuning the loose strings of the vina is there and it seems that from somewhere beyond the horizon have sounded someone's footsteps.

Swiftly come, O lovely star of dawn,
Ere the night has run its course,
Let me take my fill in wakefulness
Of the music I lost in dreams.

There is hope of redemption. The infinite undertones of the awakening universe are audible and lamp in hand, the harbinger of the Great Path is about to arrive.

Lift it from the abyss of night
And hold it for the morn,
Self-oblivious in the dark,
Make it blessed in the light.

Where the silence of sleep dissolves
In the mighty rhythm of the heavens
There let me proffer my vina—
I the half-awakened moon.

This miserable moon is myself. Early tomorrow morning I shall be off. But I want the void of my departure to be filled by the lovely morning star, with its song of awakening. What was vague and misty in the blinded dream of life shall be restored to perfect form in the light of the lovely morning star. There is in this poem the virility of hope, the luminous pride of the dawn to come, unlike the sloppy helpless ravings of your Rabindranath."

"Why be indignant, Mita? What's the use of repeating again and again that Rabindranath cannot be more than what he is?"

"You people have all conspired to make too much—"

"Don't say that, Mita. My taste is my own; is it my fault if it doesn't agree with yours or other people's? I give you my word that if ever I share that 75-rupee-a-month flat of yours, you may by all means read out your poet to me, but I shall not inflict mine on you."

"That would be unfair. Marriage means mutual submission to each other's tyranny."

"You will never stand the tyranny of taste. You will never

admit to your literary banquet any but the invited; I on the other hand will welcome all who turn up."

"Silly of me to have started this wrangle. It has spoiled the mood of this our last evening together."

"Not in the least. The mood that survives plain speaking is our true mood, the mood of inexhaustible tolerance."

"I must, however, get rid of this bad taste in my mouth. Bengali verses won't do it. English verse restores my temper best. For some time after my return to India, I was a professor."

"Our temper," laughed Labanya, "is like the bulldog in an English home, who growls at the mere sight of a dhoti, no matter who may wear it. But the sight of the bearer's livery sets its tail wagging."

"That indeed is so. Partiality is not a natural and spontaneous thing; in most cases it is made to order. From childhood partiality for English literature has been literally thrashed into us. Under the compulsion of this training we have no courage to disparage it or even to appreciate what is our own. Any way, today it shall not be Nibaran Chakravarty but cent per cent English verse without translating."

"No, no, Mita, let us defer English till we are seated at our desk at home. Let us have Nibaran Chakravarty for our last sunset together. No one else."

"Long live Nibaran Chakravarty!" exclaimed Amit exultantly. "So he has attained immortality after all. Banyâ, I shall appoint him your poet laureate. He will accept laurels at no hands but yours."

"Will that content him?"

"If it does not, I'll take him by the ear and kick him out."

"We'll decide later about ear-pulling. Now out with the poem."

Amit began to recite:

"How patiently you stayed by me,
Days and nights!
How oft your footsteps were traced
On the dusty path of my destiny!
Now that I must go far away,
Let me leave as my parting gift
A hymn of adoration to you.

How often I laboured in vain!
Life's sacred fire would not take flame.
Only despair in coils of smoke lost itself in nothingness.
How oft the flame evanescent
Painted its faint symbols

Farewell my Friend

On the forehead of the insentient night,
Ere it vanished in the untraced void of time.
    Now at your advent
The sacred fire burns proudly,
And what was futile shall now be fruitful.
To you I dedicate
My offering at the end of the day.
Accept my homage,
My life's perfect fulfilment.
Let your tender touch rest on this bowed head
At the foot of your throne
Wherever you reign in glory,
Let my adoration find a place."

13

Misgiving

It was difficult for Labanya to apply her mind to her duties the next morning. She did not go out for her usual stroll. Amit had said that he did not wish to see her in the morning before he left Shillong. She too must co-operate in that resolve and avoid the path by which Amit would have to pass. She was greatly tempted but she restrained herself. Yogamaya used to bathe early and go out to gather flowers for worship. But today Labanya left the house even earlier and came to the foot of the eucalyptus tree. In her hand she held a couple of books, perhaps intended to fool herself as well as others. The books lay open, time passed, but the leaves were never turned. The great day of life had ended yesterday, so she said to herself again and again. The morning sky was littered with patches of light and shade which every now and then were swept away by some destructive hand as with a broom. Amit, she was convinced, was a born runaway. If he slipped away, he would never be found again. He begins a romance on his wanderings, but when morning comes after the night the thread of romance is snapped and the traveller has departed. And so Labanya believed that her romance too would remain for ever incomplete. The agony of this incompleteness was reflected in the morning light and the poignancy of this premature end in the damp air.

Just then—it was nine—Amit burst into the house, shouting, "Mashima! Mashima!" Yogamaya had finished her morning worship and was busy in the pantry. She too was feeling depressed. Amit's liveliness and laughter had overflowed in her house and in her affectionate heart. The thought that he was gone weighed on her morning like heavy rain on a flower, crushing it down. She had not invited Labanya to help her in the household duties, knowing that she needed to be alone, away from other eyes.

Labanya jumped to her feet, the book fell from her lap unnoticed. Yogamaya rushed out of the pantry.

"Whatever is the matter, Amit? An earthquake?" she asked.

"Yes, an earthquake. Things all sent off—car ready—go to the Post Office for letters, and find a telegram."

Noticing the expression on Amit's face, Yogamaya asked anxiously, "I hope all is well?"

Labanya came into the room. Amit replied, visibly distressed, "My sister Cissie, with her friend Katie Mitter and Katie's brother Naren, are arriving this evening."

"What's that to worry about? I hear a house is vacant near the racecourse. If that is not available, we can easily make room for them in our house."

"That is not what is worrying me, Mashima. As a matter of fact, they have booked rooms in a hotel by telegram."

"In any case I will not let your sisters see you lodged in that wretched hovel of yours. They might hold us responsible for their brother's eccentricity."

"No, Mashima, my paradise is lost. Farewell to my unfurnished heaven! My happy dreams will fly away from their nest in my humble cot. I shall have to go too and stay in a most respectable room of this most fashionable hotel."

There was nothing much in his talk, and yet Labanya's face lost its colour. The immense distance between Amit's set and hers had never before entered her thoughts. Now it came upon her in a flash. There was no bitterness of separation in the idea of Amit leaving for Calcutta. But in his enforced removal to a hotel it was borne in upon Labanya that the invisible house their fancy had fashioned would never take visible form.

"I may go to a hotel or to hell itself," said Amit to Yogamaya, throwing a quick glance at Labanya, "but my real home is here."

Amit realized that suspicious eyes were coming from the city. His mind had turned out plan after plan to prevent Cissie and her set from coming here. But of late his letters had been coming to Yogamaya's address. It had never occurred to him that might one day prove a source of trouble.

Amit's feelings could never remain suppressed; on the contrary they found a slightly exaggerated expression. It struck Yogamaya as unseemly that he should be perturbed at the arrival of his sister. Labanya too felt that Amit was ashamed of her before his sister. It was a hateful, humiliating thought. Amit turned to Labanya, "Are you free? Can you come out for a while?"

"I am sorry," replied Labanya in a rather cold tone, "I have no time."

"Do go out for a bit, dear," pleaded Yogamaya, perturbed.

"Kartama," replied Labanya, "Surama's lessons have been badly neglected for some time. I am much to blame. Last night I made up my mind that from now on, there must be no more slackness."

Labanya's mouth was set in an obstinate line; her face was hard. Yogamaya was familiar with the symptoms—she did not dare to argue further.

"I must be off to my duty too," said Amit in a dry voice; "I must have everything ready for them."

But before he left he stood still on the veranda for a while.

"Look Banyâ," he cried, "you can see just a bit of the roof of my house through that gap in the trees. I haven't yet told you— I have bought that house. The owner was taken aback. I am sure she thought that I had found a gold mine in it. She put up the price considerably. I had discovered the gold mine all right, but I alone knew of it. The glory of my dilapidated cottage shall be hidden from all other eyes."

A shadow of deep anguish clouded Labanya's face. She said:

"Why should you mind other people so much? Let everyone know! In fact, the truth ought to be properly told, then no one would dare to be rude."

Amit made no reply to this.

"Banyâ," he said, "I've made up my mind that after our wedding we must come and stay here in that cottage. That garden of mine on the Ganges bank, the bathing ghat and the banyan tree, they are all merged in it now. The name you gave—Mitali— just suits it."

"Mita, you have left that house today. When you next want to enter it, you'll find that it is too small for you. In today's abode there is no room for tomorrow. The other day you said that man's first sadhana in life was in poverty, the second in glory. Of the final sadhana you said nothing. It's the sadhana of renunciation."

"These are your Rabindranath's words, Banyâ. He says that Shahjahan has transcended even his Taj Mahal. It never entered your poet's head that we only build in order to transcend what we have built. That is what evolution means in the creative process. Some demon seizes on us and commands. Create! Only when the creation is finished does the spirit release its hold, and then there is no longer any need for the thing created. But that does not mean that giving up is the biggest fact. There is a perennial current of Shahjahans and Mumtazes. They were not the only ones in the world. That is why the Taj has never been reduced to emptiness. Nibaran Chakravarty has written a poem on the bridal chamber, which is a terse reply—written on a post card—to your poet's ode to the Taj Mahal.

Thou shalt perforce be deserted
When the night grows unquiet
At the sound of the chariot wheels of dawn.
Alas, O Bridal Chamber,
Separation lurks, like a robber,
In the vastness without.
Yet though it breaks and tears to fragments
The garlands exchanged by lovers.
Thou art forever undestroyed,
Thy festival is never silenced nor broken.
Who says the bridal pair have forsaken thee,
Leaving desolate the nuptial bed?
They are not gone—the lovers.
In ever new guises
They return at thy call
To thy open threshold,
Coming again and again from journeyings ever new.
O Bridal Chamber,
Love is deathless,
Thou too art immortal.

Rabindranath is always harping, on the things that pass away; he doesn't know how to sing of what abides. Does the poet mean to say, Banyâ, that when we knock at that door it will not open to us?"

"I beg of you, Mita, don't start a poet's quarrel this morning. Do you think that I did not know from the very first that you are Nibaran Chakravarty? But don't begin already to build our love a monument in verse—at least wait till it dies."

Labanya knew quite well that Amit was talking at random only to suppress some inner anxiety. Amit too had realised that while the poetic combat of the previous evening was not infelicitous, this morning it sounded discordant. But the fact that Labanya too had seen through it was unpleasant to him. Somewhat dryly, he said,

"All right, I'll go. I too have my appointed task in this universe—which at the moment is to look up the hotel. It seems the luckless Nibaran Chakravarty has come to the end of his spree."

Labanya caught hold of Amit's hand and said, "Please Mita, bear with me and do not ever withhold your forgiveness. If a day comes for parting, I beg you not to leave with anger in your heart."

She hurriedly went inside to hide the tears in her eyes. For a while Amit stood rooted to the ground. Then slowly, almost absent-mindedly, he went towards the eucalyptus tree. He saw scattered there the broken walnut shells. The sight sent a strange pang to his heart. The refuse left behind by the stream of life is the more tragic because it is worthless. Then his eye fell on a book lying on the grass—Rabindranath's "Balaka". Its last leaf was wet. He thought he would go in and return the book; instead, he put it in his pocket. He thought he would go to the hotel; instead he sat down under the tree. The wet clouds of the previous night had sponged the sky clean. Everything stood out bright in the air washed clear of dust. The distant silhouette of the trees and the hills seemed to be etched on the deep blue of the sky, and the whole world seemed to have drawn close and intimate to the mind. Gradually the time passed, instinct with the music of Bhairavi.

Labanya had intended to immerse herself in her duties, but when from afar she saw Amit seated under the tree, she could restrain herself no longer, her heart felt like bursting and her eyes filled with tears. Coming up to him, she asked, "Mita, what are you thinking of?"

"The very reverse of what I have been thinking up to now."

"You are never at ease if you do not occasionally view your mind upside down. Well, tell me what the reverse of your thoughts is like."

"All along I have been building abodes for you, sometimes by the Ganges bank, sometimes in the hills. Today my mind is stirred by the vision of a path running up that hill, interspersed with wooded shade, touched with the poignant light of this morning. In my hand is a long iron-shod stick, on my shoulders a square haversack with a leather strap. You are walking by my side. Blessed be your name, that you have swept me out of the house and set me adrift. The house is crowded with other people; the road is for us two alone."

"So the garden near Diamond Harbour is gone, and that 75-rupee-a-month apartment is gone too. Very well. But how are we to keep our distance on the road? Will you spend the night in one rest house and I in another?"

"No longer necessary, Banyâ. Moving keeps one ever new at every step. There is no time to get old. Age comes with immobility."

"Why this sudden change of idea, Mita?"

"I'll tell you. I've had an unexpected letter from Sobhanlal. I dare say you have heard his name—the Premchand Roychand Scholar. He has set out on a tour to retrace the ancient routes figuring in Indian History. He wants to recover the lost routes of the past. I want to create new paths of the future."

Labanya winced as if under a sudden blow. Interrupting Amit, she said:

"Sobhanlal and I sat for our M.A. together. I should like to hear all about him."

"At one time he was obsessed with the idea of rediscovering the ancient route through Kapish in Afghanistan. Hiuen Tsang came to India as a pilgrim by that road, and before him Alexander with his army. And so Sobhanlal studied Pushtu in right earnest and the customs and laws of the Pathans. He is a handsome fellow, and in his loose trousers he looked more like a Persian than a Pathan. He insisted on my giving him letters of introduction to French savants engaged in the same research in that country. While in France I had studied under some of them. I gave him the letters, but the India Government would not grant him a passport. Since then he has been in search of a way through the inaccessible Himalayas, now in Kashmir, now in the Kumaon hills. Now he wants to try the eastern end of the Himalayas for the route of the Buddhist missions. This wanderlust of his makes me restless too. We wear out our eyes in discovering the routes of words in books, while this maniac is out to read the book of the road itself, written by the very hand of human destiny. Do you know what I think?"

"What?"

"That in his youth he must have been struck by a bangled hand, which explains his rebound from the home to the road. I do not know the full story, but one day we two were alone together and talking of various things till nearly midnight. The moon of a sudden rose into view through the flowering *jarul* tree, and he began to talk of someone. He did not tell me her name or describe her, but as soon as he began to talk about her, his voice grew thick with emotion and he hurried away. Somewhere in his life I think he has been cruelly wounded, and he wants to deaden the pain by continual marches."

Labanya, overcome by a sudden botanical zeal, bent down to examine a white-and-yellow wild flower in the grass. An imperative urge to count its petals seemed to have seized her.

"Do you know, Banyâ," Amit went on, "you have pushed me out on the road today?"

"How?"

"I built the house, but it seems from what you said this morning that you hesitate to set foot in it. For two months I had been preparing it in my mind. I called to you today. 'Come, my bride, into the house.' But you cast off the bridal robe and said, 'No, beloved, there is no room here. Our seven wedding paces shall be an endless march.' "

The botanical interest in the wild flower snapped. Labanya suddenly stood up and said in anguish, "Please Mita no more, I've no time."

The Comet

Only now did Amit discover that every Bengali in Shillong knew of his relations with Labanya. The main topic of discussion among the government clerks was the relative position of the ruling planets in the secretarial heaven. When, however, they suddenly discovered a pair of stars of the very first magnitude swim into the solar system of the human heaven, they, like good observers of celestial bodies, naturally began to discuss in all sorts of ways the fiery drama being enacted by the new luminaries.

Into the vortex of this discussion was drawn Kumar Mukherjee, an attorney who had come to the hills for a change of climate. Some had abridged his name to

Kumar Mukho, some to Mar Mukho. He was well known in the Cissie set, though he did not belong to the inner circle of her friends. Amit used to call him Mukho the Comet, for the simple reason that though he was outside their set, his tail would occasionally wag its way into their orbit. Everyone guessed that the planet which particularly drew him was known as Lissie. Everyone was amused except Lissie, who felt angry and ashamed. Accordingly she was almost always trampling violently on his tail, which fact, however, seemed to injure neither his tail nor his head.

Amit now and again caught a distant glimpse of him on the Shillong roads. It was difficult not to see him. Since he had never been outside India, his foreign ways were frantically in evidence. A long, fat cigar was constantly in his mouth, which chiefly explained his nickname, Mukho the Comet. When Amit saw him in the distance, he always tried to avoid him, and consoled himself with the delusion that the Comet was unaware of it. But to see without seeming to see is a great and subtle art. The test of skill, as in the art of thieving, is not to be found out. To overlook what is visibly evident needs the dexterity of an expert.

The extent of the information culled by Kumar Mukho from the Bengali society of Shillong might be summed up under the caption, "Amit Roy Run Riot". The greatest scandal-mongers are the greatest lovers of scandal. It was the Comet's original intention to stay for some days for the sake of his disordered liver, but a vulgar enthusiasm for spreading gossip took him back to Calcutta within five days. There in the presence of Cissie, Lissie and Co. he vomited out, along with the fumes of his cigar, terrible tales of Amit, not unmixed with farce and drollery.

The wise reader must have suspected by now that the vehicle of the goddess Cissie was Naren, Katie Mitter's elder brother. It was rumoured that he was soon to be promoted from this vehicular stage to the conjugal. Cissie was at heart willing, but pretended not to be, thereby wrapping herself in a veil of mystery. Naren had hoped that with the help of Amit's counsel he would succeed in breaking through this smoke-screen, but this humbug of an Amit would neither return to Calcutta nor answer his letter. He exhausted his vocabulary of abusive English slang by hurling it at the invisible Amit in public and in private. He even sent most uncomplimentary telegrams to Shillong, but, like a rocket fired at a star, their fiery trail was lost. In the end it was unanimously decided to investigate the matter on the spot. It was imperative that no time should be lost in hauling Amit on to the bank, if only the barest tuft of his hair were visible above the current of perdition which was sweeping him along. In this matter even more enthusiastic than his own sister Cissie was someone else's sister Katie. Katie Mitter's feeling in this respect was as strong as the resentment of our politicians at the disappearance of India's wealth into foreign lands.

Naren Mitter had lived long in Europe. Son of a Zamindar, neither earning nor spending was a problem to him; nor indeed was learning. In foreign lands he was concerned only with spending, both money and time. By styling oneself an artist one may obtain at a stroke both irresponsible freedom and unmerited self-esteem. And so in pursuit of the goddess of art he had lived in the Bohemia of every metropolis in Europe. After a short trial he had to give up painting at the earnest entreaty of his outspoken well-wishers. Since then he had been introducing himself as an art-expert, with no better claim to the title than his claim to it. If he could not improve the art of painting, he could at least confound it. The ends of his moustache were carefully pointed upwards French-fashion, and equally carefully was his shaggy hair neglected. He was handsome enough, but in the assiduous endeavour to make himself more so, he had loaded the dressing table with all sorts of Parisian beauty aids. The equipment of his washbasin would have more than sufficed even for the ten headed Ravana. Seeing that he threw away a costly Havana after a few puffs only and that he sent his clothes every month by parcel to be laundered in Paris, no one dared to question his aristocracy. His sartorial measurements were entered in the registers of the premier tailoring houses of Europe, where the names of Patiala and Kapurthala might also be found. His English was well seasoned with slang, which he minced and drawled with a sleepy, sluggish stare in his half-closed eyes. Those who knew testified that many blue-blooded nobles of England spoke in such muffled guttural tones. Moreover, his stock of horsey slang and obscene oaths made him the hero of his set.

Katie Mitter's real name was Ketaki. In the distillery of her brother's style her manners had been thrice refined—a concentrated, superfine essence of foreign make. In her spite against the average Bengali girl's pride in her long hair, she had with equal pride applied the scissors to her own, so that her hair, like the tail of a tadpole, had been transmuted into the bob of the evolved model. Her naturally fair complexion was well coated with enamel. In her childhood Katie's dark eyes had been gentle and serene, now they seemed too lofty to rest on the common-place. If by chance they did rest, they took no notice; or, they did take notice, they glittered like a half-drawn knife. Her lips, once sweet and unaffected, were set by constant sneering in the hard curve of a twisted goad. I am not competent to describe feminine attire, I am ignorant of the vocabulary. What, however, struck the eye was the extremely fine texture of the outer wear, delicate as the slough of a serpent, through which was visible the tint of the underwear. Her blouse exposed rather than covered her bust and her bare arms would rest now on a table, now on the arm of a chair, or would be posed with the utmost care in an affectation of extreme refinement. When she puffed at a cigarette held between her manicured fingers, it was less for the sake of the smoke than for the decorative effect. But the most painful part was the sophisticated gait of her high-heeled shoes. The Creator having failed to fashion the human foot on the model of the goat's hoof, this initial error in evolution was now being rectified by torturing the earth with the elevated tread of this freak of the cobbler's art.

Cissie was still in a middle state, gaining promotions fast but not yet awarded the final diploma. With her ringing laughter, incessant mirth and irrepressible chatter, she bubbled over with liveliness which her admirers found charming. She was, as Radha has been described in the bloom of her youth, now womanly and demure, now girlish and immature. Her high heels proclaimed the triumph of the changing age; the former times remained in her unshorn chignon; and while the lower end of her sari was skirted a few inches too high, its upper end was still wound with modesty. Though she carried gloves unnecessarily, she still had bangles on both wrists. Cigarettes no longer made her giddy, but the betel leaf was still very tempting; nor did she mind if she received pickles and mango preserve in a discarded biscuit tin. Of the plum pudding at Christmas and the rice-coconut sweet at the pous festival, she really preferred the latter. She had learnt ballroom dancing from a foreign teacher but was somewhat reluctant to whirl about in another's arms on a public floor.

They had all hurried to Shillong, considerably perturbed at the rumours concerning Amit, the more so as in their vocabulary Labanya was classed as a "governess"—a caste specially created to decaste men. They had no doubt whatever that she had fastened on Amit in her lust for wealth and position, and that to rescue him from her clutches would need all the ingenuity of their feminine art. The four-headed Brahma himself with his four pairs of eyes keeps ogling at the fair sex; no wonder he has made man dull-witted where woman is concerned. For this reason it is well nigh impossible for a man to extricate himself from the meshes of infatuation contrived by female strangers, without the aid of his female kith and kin who are proof against the wiles of their own sex.

In the meanwhile the two damsels arrived at an understanding between themselves as to the general plan of rescue. It was out of the question to let Amit know anything at the outset, until they had first reconnoitred the enemy forces and the field of battle and gauged the strength of the enchantress.

The very first thing that greeted their eye was the daub of rusticity of Amit. Amit, of course, had never been like the rest of his set; but he was always very urban, fastidious to a degree. Now, however, not only was his complexion tanned by life in the open but a touch of the rural seemed to have settled on his being—as though he had become green and somewhat dull-witted like the trees. He behaved almost naturally. He seemed no longer inclined to indulge in his favourite sport of pricking everything with the rapier of his laughter— which fact seemed to them an omen of an imminent disaster.

Cissie told him bluntly: "Before we came, we were afraid that you were sinking to the level of a Khasi hillman. But you are actually becoming what is called green, like the pine trees here. You may have improved in health, but are no longer so interesting."

By way of reply Amit referred her to Wordsworth's lines that the society of nature imparts to one's body, mind and spirit the character of "mute insensate things".

Said Cissie to herself, "We have no quarrel with the mute insensate things. What we are afraid of are not in the least mute, but most sweet-tongued and alert."

They had hoped that Amit would himself broach the subject of Labanya. But one day, two days, three days passed and Amit said not a word. It was, however, obvious that the boat of his heart was being tossed about a little too much. Long before they were up and about Amit would be gone somewhere, and when he returned his expression reminded one of the drooping, shredded leaves of the banana tree after a storm. Even more alarming was the discovery of one of Rabindranath's books on his bed. On the inside cover was Labanya's name, with the first two letters erased with red ink. The name was clearly the philosopher's stone which had turned the thing into gold.

Every now and again Amit would disappear—in search of appetite, as he put it. That the appetite was overwhelming was obvious, nor was it unknown to others what could appease it. But they pretended ignorance of any other appetizer in Shillong than the mountain air. Cissie laughed inwardly, Katie burned inwardly. Amit was so absorbed in his own problem that he was incapable of sensing any strain in the atmosphere. He would blandly declare that he had gone to look for a waterfall, it never occurred to him that others might wonder what kind of waterfall it was or whither its waters flowed. This morning he announced that he was going to look for orange-honey. When the girls very simply and innocently expressed their irrepressible interest in this matchless honey and offered to accompany him, Amit replied that the path was rough and inaccessible by any means of conveyance. Cutting the discussion short, he fled. Impressed by this flutter of the bee's wings, the two friends made up their minds to delay no longer and to lead an expedition that very day to the orange orchard. Naren had gone to the races. He was keen on taking Cissie with him, but she declined. What severe discipline lay behind this act of self-denial none but a feeling heart can appreciate.

15

Impediment

❧

The two friends entered the gate of Yogamaya's garden, and finding no servant about came up to the porch. They saw seated at a small table on the terrace a teacher and her pupil, engaged in study. It was easy to guess that the elder of the two was Labanya. Trotting up the steps Katie rapped out in English:

"Sorry".

"Whom do you want, please?" asked Labanya rising from her seat.

In an instant Katie's glance swept Labanya from head to foot like a sharp broom.

"We came to inquire if Mister Amitraye is here," she answered.

Labanya did not immediately grasp what kind of creature this Amitraye could be, and so she said, "We don't know him."

The two friends exchanged lightning glances, the shadow of a sneer on their faces. Katie hissed with an artery toss of her head, "We know that he often comes here—oftener than is good for him."

Labanya was taken aback. She knew now who they were and realized the mistake she had made.

"Let me call Kartama," she said embarrassed: "she will tell you all about it."

Labanya gone, Katie turned to Surama and inquired summarily,

"Your teacher?"

"Yes."

"Labanya by name, I believe?"

"Yes."

"Got matches?" asked Katie in English. Confused by this sudden switch over to the need of matches, Surama failed to grasp the meaning of the words. She stared at Katie's face.

"Matches," explained Katie in Bengali. Surama fetched a box. Lighting and smoking a cigarette, Katie asked,

"Learning English?"

Surama nodded, and then ran into the house.

"Whatever else," commented Katie, "the girl may or may not have learnt from her governess, she certainly has not learnt manners."

Between them the two friends went on with their commentary.

"The famous Labanya! Delicious! What a volcano in the Shillong hills! What an earthquake to split asunder Amit's heart! Silly! Men are funny."

Cissie laughed aloud. It was a hearty, generous laugh. For Cissie did not despise men for their follies. Why, she herself had caused earthquakes which had split the rockiest soil. But this was the limit. On one side a girl like Katie, on the other that governess in those quaint clothes who looked as though butter wouldn't melt in her mouth. What a bundle of wet rags! Sit near it and the mind gets mouldy as a biscuit in rainy weather! How could Amit ever put up with her for a moment?

"Cissie, your brother's mind is always hopping on its head. In one of his perverse, contrary moods, the girl seemed an angel no doubt."

So saying Katie rested her cigarette against the Algebra on the table and opening her silver-chained vanity bag powdered her face and repencilled her eyebrows. Cissie felt no resentment at her brother's utter lack of sense of proportion; on the contrary she felt a little touched by it. Her entire wrath was directed at the counterfeit angels who bewitched the eye of the male. Katie had no patience with Cissie's amused indifference with regard to her brother. She felt like giving her a good shake-up.

At this moment Yogamaya came out, dressed in a white silk sari. Labanya did not come. Katie had brought along her little dog Tabby whose shaggy hair overhung his eyes. He had been content with a sniffing introduction in the case of Labanya and Surama, but the sight of Yogamaya seemed to kindle more enthusiasm in his mind. He rushed up to her and lifting up his fore-paws made a declaration of his genuine love by inscribing on her clean sari his muddy autograph. Cissie dragged him by the collar to Katie. Katie tapped his nose with her forefinger. "Naughty dog!" she scolded.

Katie did not rise from her seat. Puffing at the cigarette, she turned her head and stared at Yogamaya with undisguised nonchalance. Apparently her wrath against Yogamaya was even greater than against Labanya. She imagined that Labanya's past was tainted and that it was Yogamaya who in the guise of an aunt had contrived to palm her off on Amit. It does not need any super intelligence to beguile the male. Providence having already blindfolded him.

Cissie came forward, gave Yogamaya the semblance of a greeting, and said, "I am Cissie, Amit's sister."

Yogamaya smiled and said, "Amit calls me Mashi which gives me the right, dear, to be aunt to you as well."

In view of Katie's attitude, Yogamaya took no notice of her. To Cissie she said, "Come, dear come inside."

"There's no time," replied Cissie. "I came only to inquire if Amit is here."

"He hasn't come yet," said Yogamaya.

"Do you know when he will turn up?"

"I can't say. But I will go and find out."

Without moving from her seat, Katie rapped out:

"That schoolmistress who was coaching here pretended she had never met Amit."

Yogamaya was dumbfounded. She sensed mischief. She too realised that it would not be easy to maintain one's self-respect before them. Instantly foregoing her aunthood, she remarked, "I understand Amit Babu stays in your hotel. You should know his whereabouts."

Katie laughed unpleasantly, a laugh which translated into, "You may bluff, but you can't fool us."

The fact was that Katie's temper had been inflamed at the very outset by the sight of Labanya and her assertion that she did not know who Amit was. But Cissie, though she felt concerned, was not enraged. She felt drawn by the deep calm of Yogamaya's beautiful mien, and was embarrassed when she saw Katie flagrantly slight her by not rising from her seat. On the other hand, she dared not go against Katie in any matter, for Katie was swift in crushing sedition. She brooked no opposition, and did not scruple to be nasty. Most people are timid and are cowed by brazen bullying. Katie prided herself on her unfailing ruthlessness and never spared her friends if she discovered any of them showing evidence of what she called goody-goody amiability. She paraded her rudeness under the name of frankness and those who shrank from its bludgeonings did everything to please her in the interests of peace. Cissie was one of them. The more she feared Katie in secret, the more she aped her, to prove herself no weakling. She did not always succeed.

Katie divined that some shame-faced disapproval of her conduct was lurking in a corner of Cissie's mind. These misgivings must be crushed, she decided, and in Yogamaya's presence. She got up and, thrusting a cigarette between Cissie's lips, brought her face forward to light the cigarette with her own. Cissie dared not object, though the tips of her ears were somewhat red. She forced herself to assume an expression which implied that she was ready to snap her fingers at anyone who should frown, however slightly, on western ways.

At this juncture Amit arrived. The girls were taken aback. When he had left the hotel he was wearing English dress and a felt hat; now he appeared in a dhoti and shawl: The den where he changed his costume was that cottage of his. There was his shelf of books, a trunk full of clothes and an easy chair given by Yogamaya. After lunch he left the hotel and took shelter there. Labanya was strict in her discipline nowadays, and while engaged in teaching Surama would not permit anyone to interpose in search of a waterfall or oranges. And so not before 4.30 in the afternoon, when they met for tea, had Amit access to this house, nor any permissible means of assuaging his thirst, physical and spiritual. He managed somehow to while away the time till then, when, changing his dress, he would arrive punctual to the minute.

Today the ring had arrived from Calcutta before he left

the hotel. He had been picturing in his imagination how he would put the ring on Labanya's finger. Today was a special day for him. Such a day could not be made to wait at the outer gate. Today all other work must be suspended. He had made up his mind to march straight to where Labanya would be sitting at her desk and say to her: "Once the Sovereign came riding on an elephant, but the gate was low, and rather than bend his head, he went back without entering the newly built palace. Today the great day of our life has arrived, but you have built the gate of your leisure too low. Pull it down that the King may enter your abode with his head held high." He had also thought of adding that to come at the right time might be the meaning of punctuality, but the watch's time was not true time; the watch might know the time in numbers, but how could it know its value?

Looking out, the sky had seemed grey with clouds, and the light was dim as though it was five or six in the afternoon. Amit dared not consult his watch, lest its blunt hands contradict the sky—like a mother who rejoices that her child's long-fevered body at last feels cool to the touch and who is afraid to consult the thermometer lest it belie her hopes. Today Amit arrived long before the appointed time; for hankering knows no shame.

The corner of the veranda where Labanya used to sit and teach her pupil was visible from the road. Today he saw it was empty. His heart leapt with joy. He looked at his watch at last. It was only 3.20. The other day he had told Labanya that while man is law-abiding, the gods are lawless. On earth we abide by the law in the hope that in heaven we may be worthy of the nectar of the lawless. When such a heaven appears on earth, we must honour it by breaking the law. He began to hope that perhaps Labanya too had realised the dignity of breaking the law, that she had somehow felt the breath of the Great Day and had pulled down the barriers of the commonplace.

Coming nearer he saw Yogamaya standing outside her door, like one struck and Cissie lighting her cigarette from Katie's. That the disrespect was intentional, he at once divined. Tabby, thwarted in his first spontaneous outburst of friendliness, was trying to doze at Katie's feet. At Amit's approach he began fidgeting to welcome him but Cissie gave him a sharp reminder that such an expression of goodwill would be out of place.

Amit did not even glance at the pair. "Mashi," he called, as he came up and stooped down to take the dust of Yogamaya's feet. It was never his way to pranam in this manner at this time of the day. He inquired,

"Where's Labanya, Mashima?"

"I hardly know, my son. Perhaps in her room."

"But it's not yet time for her class to be over."

"I think she retired when they arrived."

"Let's go and see what she is doing."

Amit went inside with Yogamaya, completely ignoring the presence of any other living creature.

"Insult!" cried Cissie. "Let's go home, Katie."

Katie was no less incensed, but she wanted to see the matter through.

"No good waiting," said Cissie.

"Some good shall come of it," answered Katie, her big eyes getting bigger.

Some time passed. Cissie again pleaded, "Let's go. I don't at all feel like staying longer."

But Katie would not budge from the veranda.

"He must come out this way," she said.

At last Amit came out, accompanied by Labanya. Labanya's face was radiant with peace, with not a trace of resentment, insolence or pride. Yogamaya had remained inside. She did not feel like coming out. Amit went and brought her out. Katie noticed the ring on Labanya's finger. Blood rushed to her head, her eyes became red, and she felt like kicking the very ground under her feet.

"Mashi," said Amit, "this is my sister Shamita. It seems my father wanted her name to rhyme with mine, but the verse turned out to be blank. Ketaki, my sister's friend."

In the meantime another disaster was brewing. Surama's pet cat happened to come out. This impertinence on her part seemed to Tabby's canine logic a sufficient provocation to challenge her to a combat. First he advanced growling, and then backed, scared by the upraised paws and feline snarling into a misgiving as to the issue of the battle. Finally taking his stand at a sufficient distance and finding non-violent roaring the safest expression of heroism, he launched a terrific volley of barks. Without taking up the gauntlet the cat merely arched her back and walked out. This was too much for Katie. Enraged she began to box Tabby's ears. Not a little of this fury was aimed at her own stars. The dog howled a sharp protest at this unfair treatment. The gods laughed in silence.

When the uproar subsided Amit turned to Cissie. "Cissie, this is Labanya. Though you have never heard her name from me, I dare say you have heard it from many others. We are engaged to be married in Calcutta in Agrahayana."

Katie was quick to contrive a smile.

"I congratulate," she said. "The orange-honey does not seem to have been difficult of access after all. Nor was the road rough. In fact, the honey seems to have leapt into your mouth."

Cissie giggled, as was her wont. Labanya felt the malice in the words but did not understand the allusion. Amit explained. "This morning as I came out they asked me where I was going. I replied, in search of wild honey. That's what they are laughing at. It's my fault. Others can't understand when I am serious and when I am fooling."

"Now that you have won your orange-honey," said Katie in a sobered tone, "see that I am not the loser."

"What must I do?"

"I made a bet with Naren. He said that no one could prevail on you to visit the haunts of gentlemen, that you could never be made to go to the races. I staked this diamond ring of mine that I would take you to the races. I looked for you at all the waterfalls and all the honey stalls in the district till I found you here. Didn't we have to wander a lot, Cissie, hunting the wild goose, as they say in English?"

By way of reply, Cissie giggled.

"It reminds me of that story you once told me, Amit,"

continued Katie, "about the Persian philosophy. When the thief stole his turban and he couldn't trace him, he went and sat in the graveyard. For, said he, sooner or later he must come here. I was quite taken aback when Miss Labanya said she didn't know Amit, but something told me that in the end he would have to come back to this graveyard of his."

Cissie shrieked with laughter.

"Amit didn't mention your name," said Katie to Labanya. "He talked in honeyed metaphors about orange honey. But you are much too unsophisticated for metaphors; you can't manage such tricks of speech, you simply blurted out that you didn't know Amit at all. Nor did the fates punish either of you as according to the Sunday schools they should have done. One of you laps up the inaccessible nectar with a smack, the other knows the unknown at a glance, and I am apparently the only loser! How unfair, Cissie!"

Cissie emitted another shriek of laughter. Even Tabby imagined that social etiquette called for his participation in this hilarity, and began to show signs of fidgeting. For the third time he had to be snubbed.

"You know, Amit," Katie went on, "if I lose this diamond ring I shall never have any peace. It was you who gave it to me. I have never taken it off for a single instant; it has become a part of myself. Is it to be forfeit now, after all these years, in a bet in Shillong?"

"What made you go betting with it, dear?" asked Cissie.

"Too much vanity, and too much trust in man. Well, pride goes before a fall. I have run my race and lost. It seems I can no longer please Amit. Why did you ever give me the ring—so affectionately, too—if you were going to jilt me like this? Was there nothing binding in the giving of it? No promise that you would never let me down?"

Katie's voice grew hoarse as she spoke, and with a great effort she kept back her tears.

It happened seven years ago, when Katie was eighteen. One day Amit had taken the ring off his own finger and put it on hers. They were both in England. A Punjabi youth in Oxford was head over ears in love with Katie. That day he and Amit had had a friendly rowing match on the river, and Amit had won. In the June moonlight the whole sky had grown eloquent, the gay riot of flowers in every meadow had robbed the earth of its self-possession, Amit slipped the ring on Katie's finger. Much was implied in the act, though little was secret. Katie's face was not plastered with paint in those days, her laughter was spontaneous, she could still blush. As he slipped the ring on her finger, Amit whispered:

> *"Tender is the night
> And haply the queen moon is on her throne."*

Katie had not yet learned to chatter. She drew a deep breath and murmured as though to herself, "Mon ami!"

And now even Amit had no answer ready. He did not know what to say. Katie went on:

"Since I have lost the bet, Amit, you had better keep the ring as a token of my final defeat. It shan't act as a lie on my finger any longer."

She took off the ring, threw it on the table, and hurried out. The tears poured down the enamelled cheeks.

16

Liberation

❦

A short letter from Sobhanlal reached Labanya's hands: "I arrived in Shillong last night. I should like to call on you, if you would permit me. If you don't, I shall leave tomorrow. I have been punished by you, but I have yet to understand what wrong I was guilty of and when. I have come to you today because I shall have no peace unless you tell me. Do not be afraid. I have no other favour to beg."

Labanya's eyes filled with tears; she wiped them away. She sat silent looking back on the past. She thought of the youthful fear that had caused her to suppress and crush the tender plant of love. Had she accepted and allowed the first fresh impulse of the heart to grow, it would by now have borne the flower of fulfillment. But she had been too proud of her knowledge, too preoccupied with learning, too overwhelmingly vain of her independence. The sight of her father's infatuation had made her look down on love as weakness. Now love had taken its revenge and her pride lay in the dust. What might have been once as simple as breathing or laughter was difficult now. It was no longer easy to welcome with open arms this visitor from her bygone days; it was heart-rending to turn him away. She thought of the hurt and shrinking figure of the despised Sobhanlal of those days. That was a long time ago. In what nectar had the youth's rejected love been kept so long alive? What but his own innate nobility?

Labanya wrote back:

"You are the best friend I have. I have no wealth now to repay this gift of your friendship. You never asked for return, and even today you have come to give what you have, making no claim. I have neither the vanity nor the strength to refuse your gift and turn you away."

Hardly had she dispatched the letter when Amit came in.

"Come, Banyâ," he said, "let's go out." He spoke very timidly, afraid that Labanya would not consent. But she said very simply, "Let's go."

They went out. Somewhat hesitantly Amit took Labanya's hand. She did not object and let him hold it. Amit pressed her hand rather hard. It was all the expression he could find. Words refused to come. Walking along they came to the spot they had visited before, where the glade suddenly appeared in the forest. The sun went down, leaving its last touch on the crest of a treeless hill. Delicate hues of green melted imperceptibly into the soft and tender blue. There they halted and stood facing the view.

Labanya spoke very gently.

"Why did you make me steal the ring which you once put on another's finger?"

Amit was hurt. "How can I make you understand, Banyâ?" he said. "The person on whose finger I once put the ring and the person who flung it back today—are they the same?"

"Nature's loving hand shaped one of them," answered Labanya. "and your indifference made the other."

"That's not wholly true," said Amit. "The blows that made Katie what she is were not all struck by me."

"But she once gave herself completely into your hands, Mita. Why didn't you make her your own? You loosened your hold and let her go, no matter why, and since then a dozen hands have fallen on her and made her what she is. It was because she lost you that she began to deck herself out for other tastes. That's why she looks like a foreign doll. If her heart had remained alive it couldn't have happened. But we won't talk any more about that. I want to ask you a favour, and you must say yes."

"Of course I will. What is it?"

"Take our friends for a week's trip to Cherapunji. Even if you can't make her happy, you can at least keep her amused."

"All right," said Amit after a pause.

Labanya leaned her head against Amit's breast. "I'm going to say something, Mita," she went on, "which I will never say again. The inner bond between us must not tie your hands in the slightest degree. I don't say this in anger, but in the fullness of my love. Please don't give me any ring, there is no need of any outward token. Let my love be untainted by any external mark or shadow."

She took the ring from her finger and gently put it on Amit's. Amit did not resist.

As the earth silently raises her face to heaven in the hushed beauty of twilight, in the same quietude, the same radiant peace, Labanya raised her face to Amit's.

17

The End

As soon as the seven days were over, Amit returned to Yogamaya's house. The house was closed, every one had left. There was nothing to indicate where they had gone.

Amit stood under the familiar eucalyptus tree; with a bleak heart he began to pace to and fro. The familiar gardener came and saluted and asked, "Shall I open the house? Would you like to go in?"

"Yes," replied Amit, after a slight hesitation.

He went into Labanyas' sitting room. The table, chair and shelf were there, but the books were missing. On the floor lay a couple of empty, torn envelopes with Labanya's name and address written in an unfamiliar hand. Two or three used and discarded nibs and the tiny stub of a worn-out pencil were on the table. Amit put the pencil in his pocket. The bedroom was adjacent. A mattress on the iron bedstead and an empty oil bottle on the dressing table were all it contained. Amit threw himself on the mattress, his head between his hands. The iron bed creaked. A dumb emptiness filled the room, unable to answer his questions, held in a trance that would never be broken.

Amit went to his own cottage, his body and mind limp with utter weariness. Everything was as he had left it. Even the easy-chair was there. Yogamaya had not taken it back. He understood that she had left it as her affectionate gift to him. He could almost hear her sweet, gentle voice calling to him My son! Touching the floor with his forehead, Amit did obeisance in front of the chair.

The Shillong hills were beautiful no longer. Amit could find solace nowhere.

The Last Poem

Jatishankar was in college in Calcutta, boarding in the Kalutola Presidency College Mess. Amit often took him home to dinner, read all sorts of books with him, startled his mind with all sorts of strange talk, and took him out for drives in his car.

Then for some time Jatishankar had no definite news of Amit. Sometimes he heard he was in Nainital, sometimes in Ootacamund. One day he heard a friend of Amit's jestingly remark that Amit was out to scrub the paint off Katie Mitter. He had found a task after his own heart, colour-changing. Previously he had been appeasing his creative urge with words; now he had taken in hand a living human being. As for the person concerned, she too was willing to shed the painted petals on her surface in hope of the ultimate fruit. Amit's sister Lissie had complained that Katie had changed beyond recognition, meaning that she was looking too much like her natural self. She had even asked her friends to call her Ketaki; which was shameless—the "modest maiden" overstuffed with under-garments after having paraded the semi-nudity of Santipuri muslin saris. Amit was said to call her "Keya" in private. It was even whispered that when they went boating on Nainital lake Katie took the oars and Amit read to her from Rabindranath's *Aimless Voyage*. But people will say anything. Jatishankar well understood that Amit's mind, like a boat in full sail, was swept along in the high tide of the holiday spirit.

At last Amit returned. It was rumoured that he and Ketaki were engaged to be married, though Amit himself said not a word about it to Jati. Amit's ways, too, were considerably changed. He continued to buy English books and give them to Jati, but he no longer spent the evenings with him discussing the books. Jati could guess that the current of discussion had now found a new channel. He was no longer invited to a ride in the car. At Jati's age it was not difficult to appreciate the impossibility of taking a third person on Amit's "Aimless Voyage."

Jati could restrain himself no longer. He asked Amit point-blank, "Amitda, I hear you are engaged to Miss Ketaki Mitter."

After a moment's pause Amit asked in return:

"Has Labanya heard that?"

"No, I have not written to her. Not having your word for it, I've said nothing."

"The news is true, but I am afraid Labanya will misunderstand."

Jati laughed. "What is there to misunderstand? If you marry, you marry. A simple thing."

"Look here, Jati, no language of man is simple. A word which has only one meaning in the dictionary comes to have half a dozen in the life of man, like the Ganges forking out in many streams when it nears the sea."

"In other words," remarked Jati, "you mean to suggest that marriage does not mean marriage."

"I mean to suggest that marriage has a thousand meanings.

Different meanings are revealed in different lives. Eliminate the man, and the meaning is confused."

"Well, let's have your meaning then."

"It cannot be defined. It has to be lived. If I say that in essence it means love, I run into another word—the thing called love is even more dynamic than the thing called marriage."

"In that case, Amitda there's an end to all discussion. Are we to go chasing the meaning under a load of words, while it dodges and swerves left or right as it pleases? One can't go on like that."

"Well said, brother. My company has inspired your tongue. Words are absolutely essential for carrying on the work of the world. Truths that are too big for words have to be pruned down for the business market. It is the words that count. What else is to be done? It is intellectually unsatisfactory, but we shut our eyes and get on with the job."

"Do we then abandon the discussion?"

"No harm in that, if it's merely an intellectual exercise with no vital interest involved."

"Well, assume that there is a vital interest involved."

"Hear, hear! then listen."

A brief commentary would not be out of place here. Jati nowadays often came for a cup of tea, served by Amit's youngest sister Lissie with her own hand. It is not unreasonable to conclude that that was why Jati did not in the least mind that Amit no longer engaged him in literary discussions in the afternoon, or took him out for a drive in the evening. He had forgiven Amit with all his heart.

Amit said, "Oxygen is invisibly present in the air or else no life could exist. On the other hand, it also unites with the coal in the fire which we put to so many uses. In neither form can we do without it. Do you understand now?"

"Not quite, though I should like to."

"The love that freely pervades the sky is the mate of our souls; the love that blends with each little daily act is the help-mate of our homes. I want both of them."

"I can't even make out whether I have understood you or not. Please be a little more explicit, Amitda."

Amit said, "A day was when with outspread wings I attained the heaven of my flight. Today my wings are folded; I lie in my little nest. But my heaven remains."

"But isn't it possible to have the sky-mate and the home-mate in one?"

"Happy accidents are possible but they don't usually happen. He's a lucky fellow who wins the princess and half the kingdom together. But the man who holds the kingdom by the right hand and the princess by the left, though he cannot unite them, is a pretty lucky fellow, too."

"But—"

"But it suffers in what you call romance? Not a bit.

Must we mould our romances on the pattern of the novels? By no means. I will create my own romance. One survives in my heaven, the other I shall build on earth. You call them romantic who to save one wind up the other. They must either swim in water like fish or pace the bank like cats or wander in the air like owls. I am the Paramahamsa[1] of romance. I shall realise the truth of love on land and water, and in the air as well. My nest shall be firmly lodged in an islet in the river and when I soar Manas-wards, it shall be by the limitless roads of air. Long live my Labanya! Long live my Ketaki! And blessed in every respect be Amit Roy!"

Jati sat silent looking as though he did not relish the idea. Amit smiled at his expression.

"Look here, brother," he said. "One man's meat is another man's poison. What I am saying need only apply to myself. You will misunderstand if you think it's meant for you and will only revile me. Much of the strife and confusion in the world comes of foisting one man's meaning on to another man's words. I'll try to make my own meaning

---

[1] Generally a sanyasi who has realised the Supreme Truth. The Bengali saint, Ramakrishna, who is said to have practised diverse religious techniques to attain the same highest realisation, is known as Paramahamsa. Literally the word means the Great Swan, a mythical bird supposed to float on the sacred lake Manas in the Himalayas, known as Manasarovar. Manas also means, of the mind, in the realm of imagination, etc. Hence the pun on the word, Manaswards, in the subsequent part of Amit's speech.

clear once more. I shall have to use a figure of speech to cover the shame of the naked word. What binds me to Ketaki is love, but this love is like water in a vessel, which I shall daily draw and daily use. The love which draws me to Labanya is a lake which cannot be brought indoors but in which my mind will swim."

Jati asked with a slight embarrassment:

"But, Amitda, couldn't we make a choice between the two?"

"Those who can, may, I can't."

"But what if Srimati Ketaki—"

"She knows everything. Whether she fully comprehends, I cannot say. But I shall spend my life and show that I have not cheated her in any way. She must know too that she is indebted to Labanya."

"That's all right, but Srimati Labanya must be told of your marriage."

"She shall be told without fail. But before that I want to send her a letter. Will you take it to her?"

"Yes, I'll take it."

This was Amit's letter:

That evening when we stood at the end of the road, I ended your journey with a poem. Today too I stand at the end of a road, and I want to mark this last moment with a poem. It cannot bear the weight of any other words. The unfortunate Nibaran Chakravarty, like a most delicate fish, died as soon as he was caught. And so, since there is no help for it, I leave it to your Poet to utter to you my last words:

Invisible, your image unchanging is in my eyes,
In the unseen chamber of my heart you abide for ever.
I've found the stone that turns all into gold,
The void in me you yourself have filled.
Dark was life when I discovered in the heart's shrine
The lighted lamp you had left as your parting gift.
Separation, like sacred fire, revealed in the glow of sorrow
Love's image divine.

Mita.

Some days passed. One day Ketaki had gone to the *Annaprasan* festival of her sister's daughter. Amit did not go. He was sprawling in an easy chair, with his feet on a chair in front, reading the Letters of William James, when Jatishankar brought a letter from Labanya. On one side of the sheet was the news of Labanya's wedding to Sobhanlal six months later, in the month of June, on the Ramgarh Hills. On the other side:

Farewell my Friend

Can you hear the wheels of Time
Rolling in ceaseless motion
On the breast of darkness where stars
Like gaping wounds wail
And the human hearts wake up in fear?
Dear friend, these ruthless wheels
Have torn me from your side
And flung me far away,
Across a thousand deaths,
On the peak of a strange dawn.

What I was is whirled away
In the dust of time,
And no way is left for return.
Could you see you would not know me now—
My friend, farewell.
And yet in the respite
Of an idle day in Spring,
When the fallen bakul flowers
Raise their moan to the sky,
And a sigh from the forgotten past
Rustles through your being,
May be, if you look within you'll see

A bit of me clinging to some corner of your mind,
Revealing a forgotten twilight,
Giving shape to a nameless dream.

No, not a dream!
The supreme truth of my being this,
My Love, death-conquering,
My gift to you imperishable, unchanging.
Let me be borne away
By the changing tide—
The gift remains.
My friend, farewell.

No loss is yours in losing me,
An image of clay.
If of that mortal dust
You have fashioned a goddess,
Let the goddess remain for you to adore
With the evening star.
No gross touch of the actual me
Shall disturb the play of your worship,
No hot breath of passionate ardour
Sully its flowers consecrate.

Farewell my Friend

To the rich repast of your fancies
I shall not come with my earthen bowl
Wet with hungry tears.
Who knows, even now your words may fashion
Out of the fragments
Of what remains of me in your memory
A new creation dream-enchanted,
That weighs not as a burden
Nor makes claims.
My friend, farewell.

Grieve not on my account,
Wide is the world and many its tasks.
My cup of life not yet discarded
Shall fill again-
Let this faith sustain me ever.
I may yet be blest
If there be one whose anxious, eager heart
Waits for my footsteps.
I long to give myself to him
Who can see in the infinite compassion of love
The actual me, of good and ill blended,
Who can make the dark night gracious
With flowers plucked in the moonlight.

What I gave to you Is yours by right everlasting.
What others receive
Are the daily driblets the heart yields
To tender solicitude
O my princely, peerless friend,
What I gave to you was your own gift—
Fuller your acceptance, the deeper my debt,
My friend, farewell.

Banyâ.